KEEP THE FAITH, BABY...

"Keep faith with me, barbarian!" the were-woman Lilitu demanded. "I have kept faith with you. I have led you where never living man has trod, and brought you forth unharmed. I have betrayed the dwellers in darkness and done that for which the goddess Tiamat will bind me naked on a white-hot grid for seven times seven days. Speak the words and free my mate from the spell that imprisons him!"

Pyrrhas spoke the incantation. With a loud sigh of relief, the were-man rose from the floor. While the barbarian stood with his hand on his sword and his head bent, lost in moody thought, Lilitu's eyes flashed a quick meaning to her mate. Lithely they began to steal toward the abstracted man.

Some primitive instinct brought his head up with a jerk. They were closing in on him, their eyes burning in the moonlight, their fingers reaching for him. Instantly he realized his mistake; he had forgotten to make the were-creatures swear truce with him before releasing the spell. No oath bound them from his flesh....

—from "The House of Arabu"

THE ROBERT E. HOWARD LIBRARY

Cormac Mac Art
Kull
Solomon Kane
Bran Mak Morn
Eons of the Night

Forthcoming:
Trails in Darkness
Beyond the Borders

EONS OF THE NIGHT

ROBERT E. HOWARD

BAEN

CONTENTS

ACKNOWLEDGMENTS

"The House of Arabu," copyright 1951, under title "The Witch from Hell's Kitchen," by Avon Novels, Inc. for *Avon Fantasy Reader*, Number 18.

"The Garden of Fear," copyright 1934 by Fantasy Publications for *Marvel Tales*, July-August 1934.

"The Twilight of the Grey Gods," copyright 1962, under title "The Grey God Passes," by August Derleth for *Dark Mind, Dark Heart*.

"Spear and Fang," copyright 1925 by Popular Fiction Publishing Company for *Weird Tales*, July 1925.

"Delenda Est," copyright 1968 by Galaxy Publishing Corporation for *Worlds of Fantasy*, Volume 1, Number 1.

"Marchers of Valhalla," copyright 1972 by Glenn Lord for *Marchers of Valhalla*.

"Sea Curse," copyright 1928 by Popular Fiction Publishing Company for *Weird Tales*, May 1928.

"Out of the Deep," copyright 1967 by Health Knowledge, Inc. for *Magazine of Horror*, November 1967.

"In the Forest of Villefère," copyright 1925 by Popular Fiction Publishing Company for *Weird Tales*, August 1925.

"Wolfshead," copyright 1926 by Popular Fiction Publishing Company for *Weird Tales*, April 1926.

ROBERT E. HOWARD

Robert E. Howard is one of the best known and most underestimated writers of the fantasy and pulp-adventure genres. A Texan who rarely left his hometown of Cross Plains and died there by his own hand in 1936, his tales of lost races, prehistoric adventure, Oriental derring-do and Cowboy/Western action spanned continents and millenia. He is best known for his tales of Conan, a barbarian adventurer who lived and wandered in the Hyborian Age—a mythical period between the sinking of Atlantis and the beginnings of recorded history, when land and sea took different shapes, a time of gleaming cities, savage wilderness, and powerful magicians.

In fact, Conan has been the nemesis of Howard's literary reputation, largely because of the enormous spin-off industry of other writers producing Conan pastiche. To many, Howard is the embarrassing essence of "pulp," overwritten and overblown.

Even on a technical reading of Howard's prose, this is unfair. Granted, he is no Proust, although if you compare him to his contemporaries—the other writers for pulp magazines such as *Weird Tales* or *Oriental Adventures*—you might think so. In fact, he usually writes a straightforward transparent style, surprisingly sparing of adjectives. Many of his descriptive passages are hauntingly beautiful.

Moreover, Howard was an innovator of some note. Before him, the field of exotic adventure was largely undifferentiated. A writer might set tales of derring-do in historical times, in out of the way places—areas still unexplored, such as Africa, Central Asia—or on another world. They might include additional wonders in the form of exotic animals, super-science, mental powers or outright magic. Rider Haggard, Burroughs, Kline and Mundy were among those who penned such tales, but there was no genre of fantasy or heroic fantasy as such.

It was Robert E. Howard who first—almost by accident—produced heroic fantasy as it is understood today, a reasonably coherent created world (in his case set in the mythical past), complete with an invented set of nations, a history, religions, gods, demons, flora and fauna, and a system of working magic . . . and a map. These are the clichés of the endless flood of fantasies which weigh down the shelves of bookstores in our day, but in Howard's the whole concept was strikingly novel. So too was Howard's preference for barbarians as heroes.

Few novels of fantasy were written in Howard's day; genre fiction was overwhelmingly in short-story or novella form, in the motley collection of magazine known as the pulps. Most of their contents were as lurid as their covers. Howard's tales were as high colored as any, but far better written than most. . . .

—**S. M. Stirling**

INTRODUCTION

I was eighteen when I wrote "Spear and Fang," "The Lost Race," "The Hyena"; nineteen when I wrote "In the Forest of Villefère" and "Wolfshead." And after that it was two solid years before I sold another line of fiction. I don't like to think about those two years. I wrote my first professional story when I was fifteen, and sent it—to *Adventure*, I believe. Three years later I managed to break into *Weird Tales*. Three years of writing without selling a blasted line. (I never have been able to sell to *Adventure;* guess my first attempt cooked me with them forever!) I haven't been any kind of a success, financially, though I have managed to get by. I could have studied law, or gone into some other occupation, but none offered me the freedom writing did—and my passion for freedom is almost an obsession. I honestly have paid the price of freedom by living with Spartan simplicity, and doing without things I really wanted. Of course, I've always hoped to some day make more than a bare living out of the game, and I was beginning to do that, when the markets started cracking up.

Writing has always been a means to an end I hoped to achieve: freedom. Personal liberty may be a phantom, but I hardly think anyone would deny that there is more liberty in writing than there is in slaving in an iron foundry, or working— as I have worked—from twelve to fourteen hours, seven days out of the week, behind a soda fountain. I have worked as much as eighteen hours a day at my typewriter, but it was work of my own choosing, and I could quit any time I wanted to without getting fired from the job. Yes, writing has been more of a means to an end than it may be with some, but it is not to be thought that I have any contempt for it. Is it likely that I would despise a profession to which I have devoted the best years of my youth, and which I expect to follow the rest of my life? When I said that writing is merely a means of making a living, for me, I spoke the truth; but I hope I am good enough workman to enjoy my trade, and to take a proper pride in it. Just because I use the profession as a means of support does not necessarily mean that I despise it.

I was first to light a torch of literature in this part of the country, however small, frail, and easily extinguished that flame may be. I am, in my way, a pioneer. To the best of my knowledge I am the first writer to be produced by a section of country comprising a territory equal to that of the state of

Connecticut. In the last few years large numbers of youngsters have taken to writing; some of them show real merit; some have already far surpassed me. But I was the first writer of the post oak country; my work's lack of merit can not erase that fact. By first, I do not, of course, mean in point of excellence, God knows; I mean in point of time. There are some real writers growing up in this country now, whose work will be read and applauded long after my junk has passed to the oblivion it will earn. But when I set my hand to my chosen profession, there was none other in the land except me. At least, if there was, I never heard of him.

It seems to me that many writers, by virtue of environments of culture, art, and education, slip into writing because of their environments. I became a writer in spite of my environments. Understand, I am not criticizing those environments. They were good, solid, and worthy. The fact that they were not inducive to literature and art is nothing in their disfavor. Nevertheless it is no light thing to enter into a profession absolutely foreign and alien to the people among which one's lot is cast; a profession which seems as dim and far-away and unreal as the shores of Europe. The people among which I lived—and yet live, mainly—made their living from cotton, wheat, cattle, oil, with the usual percentage of businessmen and professional men. That is most certainly not in their disfavor. But the idea of a man making his living by writing seemed, in that hardy environment, so fantastic that even today I am sometimes myself assailed by a feeling of unreality. Nevertheless, at the age of fifteen, having never seen a writer, a poet, a publisher, or a magazine editor, and having only the vaguest ideas of procedure, I began working on the profession I had chosen. I have accomplished little enough, but such as it is, it is the result of my own efforts. I had neither expert aid nor advice. I studied no courses in writing; until a year or so ago, I never read a book by anyone advising writers how to write. Ordinarily I had no access to public libraries, and when I did, it was to no such libraries as exist in the cities. Until recently I employed no agent. I have not been a success, and probably never will be. But whatever my failure, I have this thing to remember: that I was pioneer in my profession just as my grandfathers were in theirs, in that I was the first man in this section to earn his living as a writer.

—**Robert E. Howard**

*From a letter to H. P. Lovecraft,
Cross Plains, Texas, 1933*

Howard lived during the golden age of archaeology, when the Western world first gained extensive knowledge of the primal civilizations of Mesopotamia—of Sumer, Akkad, and Ur of the Chaldees. He read widely in the new discoveries, mining them for settings and themes and combining them with his own idiosyncratic viewpoints. This story of treachery, magic, and intrigue among the Sumerians has many of Howard's favorite themes: the giant yellow-haired barbarian wanderer, the treacherous dancing-girl, and the unspeakable demonic presence lurking in the ruins outside the walls of men.

THE HOUSE OF ARABU

To the house whence no one issues,
To the road from whence there is no return,
To the house whose inhabitants are deprived of light,
The place where dust is their nourishment, their food clay,
They have no light, dwelling in dense darkness,
And they are clothed, like birds, in a garment of feathers,
Where, over gate and bolt, dust is scattered.
—BABYLONIAN LEGEND OF ISHTAR

"Has he seen a night-spirit, is he listening to the whispers of them who dwell in darkness?"

Strange words to be murmured in the feast-hall of Naram-ninub, amid the strain of lutes, the patter of fountains, and the tinkle of women's laughter.

The great hall attested the wealth of its owner, not only by its vast dimensions, but by the richness of its adornment. The glazed surface of the walls offered a bewildering variegation of colors—blue, red, and orange enamels set off by squares of hammered gold. The air was heavy with incense, mingled with the fragrance of exotic blossoms from the gardens without. The feasters, silk-robed nobles of Nippur, lounged on satin cushions, drinking wine poured from alabaster vessels, and caressing the painted and bejeweled playthings which Naram-ninub's wealth had brought from all parts of the East.

There were scores of these; their white limbs twinkled as they danced, or shone like ivory among the cushions where they sprawled. A jeweled tiara caught in a burnished mass of night-black hair, a gem-crusted armlet of massive gold, earrings of carven jade—these were their only garments. Their fragrance was dizzying. Shameless in their dancing, feasting and lovemaking, their light laughter filled the hall in waves of silvery sound.

On a broad cushion-piled dais reclined the giver of the feast, sensuously stroking the glossy locks of a lithe Arabian who had stretched herself on her supple belly beside him. His appearance of sybaritic languor was belied by the vital sparkling of his dark eyes as he surveyed his guests. He was thick-bodied, with a short blue-black beard: a Semite—one of the many drifting yearly into Shumir.

With one exception his guests were Shumirians, shaven of chin and head. Their bodies were padded with rich living, their features smooth and placid. The exception among them stood out in startling contrast. Taller than they, he had none of their soft sleekness. He was made with the economy of relentless Nature. His physique was of the primitive, not of the civilized athlete. He was an incarnation of Power, raw, hard, wolfish—in the sinewy limbs, the corded neck, the great arch of the breast, the broad hard shoulders. Beneath his tousled golden mane his eyes were like blue ice. His strongly chiselled features reflected the wildness his frame suggested. There was about him nothing of the measured leisure of the other guests, but a ruthless directness in his every action. Whereas they sipped, he drank in great gulps. They nibbled at tid-bits, but he seized whole joints in his fingers and tore at the meat with his teeth. Yet his brow was shadowed, his expression moody. His magnetic eyes were introspective. Wherefore Prince Ibi-Engur lisped again in Naram-ninub's ear: "Has the lord Pyrrhas heard the whispering of night-things?"

Naram-ninub eyed his friend in some worriment. "Come, my lord," said he, "you are strangely distraught. Has any here done aught to offend you?"

Pyrrhas roused himself as from some gloomy meditation and shook his head. "Not so, friend; if I seem distracted it is because of a shadow that lies over my own mind." His accent was barbarous, but the timbre of his voice was strong and vibrant.

The others glanced at him in interest. He was Eannatum's general of mercenaries, an Argive whose saga was epic.

"Is it a woman, lord Pyrrhas?" asked Prince

Enakalli with a laugh. Pyrrhas fixed him with his gloomy stare and the prince felt a cold wind blowing on his spine.

"Aye, a woman," muttered the Argive. "One who haunts my dreams and floats like a shadow between me and the moon. In my dreams I feel her teeth in my neck, and I wake to hear the flutter of wings and the cry of an owl."

A silence fell over the group on the dais. Only in the great hall below rose the babble of mirth and conversation and the tinkling of lutes, and a girl laughed loudly, with a curious note in her laughter.

"A curse is upon him," whispered the Arabian girl. Naram-ninub silenced her with a gesture, and was about to speak, when Ibi-Engur lisped: "My lord Pyrrhas, this has an uncanny touch, like the vengeance of a god. Have you done aught to offend a deity?"

Naram-ninub bit his lip in annoyance. It was well known that in his recent campaign against Erech, the Argive had cut down a priest of Anu in his shrine. Pyrrhas' maned head jerked up and he glared at Ibi-Engur as if undecided whether to attribute the remark to malice or lack of tact. The prince began to pale, but the slim Arabian rose to her knees and caught at Naram-ninumb's arm.

"Look at Belibna!" She pointed at the girl who had laughed so wildly an instant before.

Her companions were drawing away from this girl apprehensively. She did not speak to them, or seem to see them. She tossed her jeweled head and her shrill laughter rang through the feast-hall. Her slim body swayed back and forth, her bracelets clanged and jangled together as she tossed up her white arms. Her dark eyes gleamed with a wild light, her red lips curled with her unnatural mirth.

"The hand of Arabu is on her," whispered the Arabian uneasily.

"Belibna!" Naram-ninub called sharply. His only answer was another burst of wild laughter, and the girl cried stridently: "To the home of darkness, the dwelling of Irhalla; to the road whence there is no return; oh, Apsu, bitter is thy wine!" Her voice snapped in a terrible scream, and bounding from among her cushions, she leaped up on the dais, a dagger in her hand. Courtesans and guests shrieked and scrambled madly out of her way. But it was at Pyrrhas the girl rushed, her beautiful face a mask of fury. The Argive caught her wrist, and the abnormal strength of madness was futile against the barbarian's iron thews. He tossed her from him, and down the cushion-strewn steps, where she lay in a crumpled heap, her own dagger driven into her heart as she fell.

The hum of conversation which had ceased suddenly, rose again as the guards dragged away the body, and the painted dancers came back to their cushions. But Pyrrhas turned and taking his wide crimson cloak from a slave, threw it about his shoulders.

"Stay, my friend," urged Naram-ninub. "Let us now allow this small matter to interfere with our revels. Madness is common enough."

Pyrrhas shook his head irritably. "Nay, I'm weary of swilling and gorging. I'll go to my own house."

"Then the feasting is at an end," declared the

Semite, rising and clapping his hands. "My own litter shall bear you to the house the king has given you—nay, I forgot you scorn to ride on other men's backs. Then I shall myself escort you home. My lords, will you accompany us?"

"Walk, like common men?" stuttered Prince Urilishu. "By Enlil, I will come. It will be a rare novelty. But I must have a slave to bear the train of my robe, lest it trail in the dust of the street. Come, friends, let us see the lord Pyrrhas home, by Ishtar!"

"A strange man," Ibi-Engur lisped to Libit-ishbi, as the party emerged from the spacious palace, and descended the broad tiled stair, guarded by bronze lions. "He walks the streets, unattended, like a very tradesman."

"Be careful," murmured the other. "He is quick to anger, and he stands high in the favor of Eannatum."

"Yet even the favored of the king had best beware of offending the god Anu," replied Ibi-Engur in an equally guarded voice.

The party were proceeding leisurely down the broad white street, gaped at by the common folk who bobbed their shaven heads as they passed. The sun was not long up, but the people of Nippur were well astir. There was much coming and going between the booths where the merchants spread their wares: a shifting panorama, woven of craftsmen, tradesmen, slaves, harlots, and soldiers in copper helmets. There went a merchant from his warehouse, a staid figure in sober woolen robe and white mantle; there hurried a slave in a linen tunic; there minced a painted hoyden whose short slit skirt displayed her sleek flank at every step. Above them the blue of sky whitened with the heat of the mounting sun. The glazed surfaces of the buildings shimmered. They were flat-roofed, some of them three or four stories high. Nippur was a city of sun-dried brick, but its facings of enamel made it a riot of bright color.

Somewhere a priest was chanting: "Oh, Babbar, righteousness lifteth up to thee its head—"

Pyrrhas swore under his breath. They were passing the great temple of Enlil, towering up three hundred feet in the changeless blue sky.

"The towers stand against the sky like part of it," he swore, raking back a damp lock from his forehead. "The sky is enameled, and this is a world made by man."

"Nay, friend," demurred Naram-ninub. "Ea built the world from the body of Tiamat."

"I say men built Shumir!" exclaimed Pyrrhas, the wine he had drunk shadowing his eyes. "A flat land—a very banquet-board of a land—with rivers and cities painted upon it, and a sky of blue enamel over it. By Ymir, I was born in a land the gods built! There were great blue mountains, with valleys lying like long shadows between, and snow peaks glittering in the sun. Rivers rush foaming down the cliffs in everlasting tumult, and the broad leaves of the trees shake in the strong winds."

"I, too, was born in a broad land, Pyrrhas," answered the Semite. "By night the desert lies white and awful beneath the moon, and by day it stretches in brown infinity beneath the sun. But it is in the swarming cities of men, these hives of bronze and gold and enamel and humanity, that wealth and glory lie."

Pyrrhas was about to speak, when a loud wailing attracted his attention. Down the street came a procession, bearing a carven and painted litter on which lay a figure hidden by flowers. Behind came a train of young women, their scanty garments rent, their black hair flowing wildly. They beat their naked bosoms and cried: *"Ailanu!* Thammuz is dead!" The throngs in the street took up the shout. The litter passed, swaying on the shoulders of the bearers; among the high-piled flowers shone the painted eyes of a carven image. The cry of the worshippers echoed down the street, dwindling in the distance.

Pyrrhas shrugged his mighty shoulders. "Soon they will be leaping and dancing and shouting, 'Adonis is living!', and the wenches who howl so bitterly now will give themselves to men in the streets for exultation. How many gods are there, in the devil's name?"

Naram-ninub pointed to the great zikkurat of Enlil, brooding over all like the brutish dream of a mad god.

"See ye the seven tiers: the lower black, the next of red enamel, the third blue, the fourth orange, the fifth yellow, while the sixth is faced with silver, and the seventh with pure gold which flames in the sunlight? Each stage in the temple symbolizes a deity: the sun, the moon, and the five planets Enlil and his tribe have set in the skies for their emblems. But Enlil is greater than all, and Nippur is his favored city."

"Greater than Anu?" muttered Pyrrhas,

remembering a flaming shrine and a dying priest that gasped an awful threat.

"Which is the greatest leg of a tripod?" parried Naram-ninub.

Pyrrhas opened his mouth to reply, then recoiled with a curse, his sword flashing out. Under his very feet a serpent reared up, its forked tongue flickering like a jet of red lightning.

"What is it, friend?" Naram-ninub and the princes stared at him in surprise.

"What is it?" He swore. "Don't you see that snake under your very feet? Stand aside and give me a clean swing at it—"

His voice broke off and his eyes clouded with doubt.

"It's gone," he muttered.

"I saw nothing," said Naram-ninub, and the others shook their heads, exchanging wondering glances.

The Argive passed his hand across his eyes, shaking his head.

"Perhaps it's the wine," he muttered. "Yet there was an adder, I swear by the heart of Ymir. I am accursed."

The others drew away from him, glancing at him strangely.

There had always been a restlessness in the soul of Pyrrhas the Argive, to haunt his dreams and drive him out on his long wanderings. It had brought him from the blue mountains of his race, southward into the fertile valleys and sea-fringing plains where rose the huts of the Mycenæans; thence into the isle of Crete, where, in a rude town of rough stone and wood, a swart fishing people bartered with the ships of Egypt; by those ships he had gone into Egypt, where men toiled beneath the lash to rear the first pyramids, and where, in the ranks of the white-skinned mercenaries, the Shardana, he learned the arts of war. But his wanderlust drove him again across the sea, to a mud-walled trading village on the coast of Asia, called Troy, whence he drifted southward into the pillage and carnage of Palestine where the original dwellers in the land were trampled under by the barbaric Canaanites out of the East. So by devious ways he came at last to the plains of Shumir, where city fought city, and the priests of a myriad rival gods intrigued and plotted, as they had done since the dawn of Time, and as they did for centuries after, until the rise of an obscure frontier town called Babylon exalted its city-god Merodach above all others as Bel-Marduk, the conqueror of Tiamat.

The bare outline of the saga of Pyrrhas the Argive is weak and paltry; it can not catch the echoes of the thundering pageantry that rioted through that Saga: the feasts, revels, wars, the crash and splintering of ships and the onset of chariots. Let it suffice to say that the honor of kings was given to the Argive, and that in all Mesopotamia there was no man so feared as this golden-haired barbarian whose war-skill and fury broke the hosts of Erech on the field, and the yoke of Erech from the neck of Nippur.

From a mountain hut to a palace of jade and ivory Pyrrhas' saga had led him. Yet the dim half-animal dreams that had filled his slumber when he lay as a youth on a heap of wolfskins in his shaggy-headed father's hut were nothing so strange and monstrous as the dreams that haunted him on the silken couch in the palace of turquoise-towered Nippur.

It was from these dreams that Pyrrhas woke suddenly. No lamp burned in his chamber and the moon was not yet up, but the starlight filtered dimly through the casement. And in this radiance something moved and took form. There was the vague outline of a lithe form, the gleam of an eye. Suddenly the night beat down oppressively hot and still. Pyrrhas heard the pound of his own blood through his veins. Why fear a woman lurking in his chamber? But no woman's form was ever so pantherishly supple; no woman's eyes ever burned so in the darkness. With a gasping snarl he leaped from his couch and his sword hissed as it cut the air—but only the air. Something like a mocking laugh reached his ears, but the figure was gone.

A girl entered hastily with a lamp.

"Amytis! I saw *her!* It was no dream, this time! She laughed at me from the window!"

Amytis trembled as she set the lamp on an ebony table. She was a sleek sensuous creature, with long-lashed, heavy-lidded eyes, passionate lips, and a wealth of lustrous black curly locks. As she stood there naked the voluptuousness of her figure would have stirred the most jaded debauchee. A gift from Eannatum, she hated Pyrrhas, and he knew it, but found an angry gratification in possessing her. But now her hatred was drowned in her terror.

"It was Lilitu!" she stammered. "She has

marked you for her own! She is the night-spirit, the mate of Ardat Lili. They dwell in the House of Arabu. You are accursed!"

His hands were bathed with sweat; molten ice seemed to be flowing sluggishly through his veins instead of blood.

"Where shall I turn? The priests hate and fear me since I burned Anu's temple."

"There is a man who is not bound by the priest-craft, and could aid you," she blurted out.

"Then tell me!" He was galvanized, trembling with eager impatience. "His name, girl! His name!"

But at this sign of weakness, her malice returned; she had blurted out what was in her mind, in her fear of the supernatural. Now all the vindictiveness in her was awake again.

"I have forgotten," she answered insolently, her eyes glowing with spite.

"Slut!" Gasping with the violence of his rage, he dragged her across a couch by her thick locks. Seizing his sword-belt he wielded it with savage force, holding down the writhing naked body with his free hand. Each stroke was like the impact of a drover's whip. So mazed with fury was he, and she so incoherent with pain, that he did not at first realize that she was shrieking a name at the top of her voice. Recognizing this at last, he cast her from him, to fall in a whimpering heap on the mat-covered floor. Trembling and panting from the excess of his passion, he threw aside the belt and glared down at her.

"Gimil-ishbi, eh?"

"Yes!" she sobbed, grovelling on the floor in her

excruciating anguish. "He was a priest of Enlil, until he turned diabolist and was banished. Ahhh, I faint! I swoon! Mercy! Mercy!"

"And where shall I find him?" he demanded.

"In the mound of Enzu, to the west of the city. Oh, Enlil, I am flayed alive! I perish!"

Turning from her, Pyrrhas hastily donned his garments and armor, without calling for a slave to aid him. He went forth, passed among his sleeping servitors without waking them, and secured the best of his horses. There were perhaps a score in all in Nippur, the property of the king and his wealthier nobles; they had been bought from the wild tribes far to the north, beyond the Caspian, whom in a later age men called Scythians. Each steed represented an actual fortune. Pyrrhas bridled the great beast and strapped on the saddle— merely a cloth pad, ornamented and richly worked.

The soldiers at the gate gaped at him as he drew rein and ordered them to open the great bronze portals, but they bowed and obeyed without question. His crimson cloak flowed behind him as he galloped through the gate.

"Enlil!" swore a soldier. "The Argive has drunk overmuch of Naram-ninub's Egyptian wine."

"Nay," responded another; "did you see his face that it was pale, and his hand that it shook on the rein? The gods have touched him, and perchance he rides to the House of Arabu."

Shaking their helmeted heads dubiously, they listened to the hoof-beats dwindling away in the west.

North, south and east from Nippur, farm-huts, villages and palm groves clustered the plain, threaded by the net-works of canals that connected the rivers. But westward the land lay bare and silent to the Euphrates, only charred expanses telling of former villages. A few moons ago raiders had swept out of the desert in a wave that engulfed the vineyards and huts and burst against the staggering walls of Nippur. Pyrrhas remembered the fighting along the walls, and the fighting on the plain, when his sally at the head of his phalanxes had broken the besiegers and driven them in headlong flight back across the Great River. Then the plain had been red with blood and black with smoke. Now it was already veiled in green again as the grain put forth its shoots, uncared for by man. But the toilers who had planted that grain had gone into the land of dusk and darkness.

Already the overflow from more populous districts was seeping back into the man-made waste. A few months, a year at most, and the land would again present the typical aspect of the Mesopotamian plain, swarming with villages, checkered with tiny fields that were more like gardens than farms. Man would cover the scars man had made, and there would be forgetfulness, till the raiders swept again out of the desert. But now the plain lay bare and silent, the canals choked, broken and empty.

Here and there rose the remnants of palm groves, the crumbling ruins of villas and country palaces. Further out, barely visible under the stars, rose the mysterious hillock known as the mound of Enzu—the moon. It was not a natural hill, but whose hands had reared it and for what reason none knew. Before Nippur was built it had risen above the plain, and the nameless fingers that shaped it had vanished in the dust of time. To it Pyrrhas turned his horse's head.

And in the city he had left, Amytis furtively left his palace and took a devious course to a certain secret destination. She walked rather stiffly, limped, and frequently paused to tenderly caress her person and lament over her injuries. But limping, cursing, and weeping, she eventually reached her destination, and stood before a man whose wealth and power was great in Nippur. His glance was an interrogation.

"He has gone to the Mound of the Moon, to speak with Gimil-ishbi," she said.

"Lilitu came to him again tonight," she shuddered, momentarily forgetting her pain and anger. "Truly he is accursed."

"By the priests of Anu?" His eyes narrowed to slits.

"So he suspects."

"And you?"

"What of me? I neither know nor care."

"Have you ever wondered why I pay you to spy upon him? " he demanded.

She shrugged her shoulders. "You pay me well; that is enough for me."

"Why does he go to Gimil-ishbi?"

"I told him the renegade might aid him against Lilitu."

Sudden anger made the man's face darkly sinister.

"I thought you hated him."

She shrank from the menace in the voice. "I spoke of the diabolist before I thought, and then he forced me to speak his name; curse him, I will not sit with ease for weeks!" Her resentment rendered her momentarily speechless.

The man ignored her, intent on his own somber meditations. At last he rose with sudden determination.

"I have waited too long," he muttered, like one speaking his thoughts aloud. "The fiends play with him while I bite my nails, and those who conspire with me grow restless and suspicious. Enlil alone knows what counsel Gimil-ishbi will give. When the moon rises I will ride forth and seek the Argive on the plain. A stab unaware—he will not suspect until my sword is through him. A bronze blade is surer than the powers of Darkness. I was a fool to trust even a devil."

Amytis gasped with horror and caught at the velvet hangings for support.

"You? *You?*" Her lips framed a question too terrible to voice.

"Aye!" He accorded her a glance of grim amusement. With a gasp of terror she darted through the curtained door, her smarts forgotten in her fright.

Whether the cavern was hollowed by man or by Nature, none ever knew. At least its walls, floor and ceiling were symmetrical and composed of blocks of greenish stone, found nowhere else in that level land. Whatever its cause and origin, man occupied it now. A lamp hung from the rock roof, casting a weird light over the chamber and the bald pate of the man who sat crouching over a parchment scroll on a stone table before him. He looked up as a quick sure footfall sounded on the stone steps that led down into his abode. The next instant a tall figure stood framed in the doorway.

The man at the stone table scanned this figure with avid interest. Pyrrhas wore a hauberk of black leather and copper scales; his brazen greaves glinted in the lamplight. The wide crimson cloak, flung loosely about him, did not enmesh the long hilt that jutted from its folds. Shadowed by his horned bronze helmet, the Argive's eyes gleamed icily. So the warrior faced the sage.

Gimil-ishbi was very old. There was no leaven of Semitic blood in his withered veins. His bald head was round as a vulture's skull, and from it his great nose jutted like the beak of a vulture. His eyes were oblique, a rarity even in a pure-blooded Shumirian, and they were bright and black as beads. Whereas Pyrrhas' eyes were all depth, blue deeps and changing clouds and shadows, Gimil-ishbi's eyes were opaque as jet, and they never changed. His mouth was a gash whose smile was more terrible than its snarl.

He was clad in a simple black tunic, and his feet, in their cloth sandals, seemed strangely deformed. Pyrrhas felt a curious twitching between his shoulder-blades as he glanced at those feet, and he drew his eyes away, and back to the sinister face.

"Deign to enter my humble abode, warrior," the voice was soft and silky, sounding strange from those harsh thin lips. "I would I could offer you food and drink, but I fear the food I eat and the wine I drink would find little favor in your sight." He laughed softly as at an obscure jest.

"I come not to eat or to drink," answered Pyrrhas

abruptly, striding up to the table. "I come to buy a charm against devils."

"To buy?"

The Argive emptied a pouch of gold coins on the stone surface; they glistened dully in the lamp-light. Gimil-ishbi's laugh was like the rustle of a serpent through dead grass.

"What is this yellow dirt to me? You speak of devils, and you bring me dust the wind blows away."

"Dust?" Pyrrhas scowled. Gimil-ishbi laid his hand on the shining heap and laughed; somewhere in the night an owl moaned. The priest lifted his hand. Beneath it lay a pile of yellow dust that gleamed dully in the lamplight. A sudden wind rushed down the steps, making the lamp flicker, whirling up the golden heap; for an instant the air was dazzled and spangled with the shining parti-cles. Pyrrhas swore; his armor was sprinkled with yellow dust; it sparkled among the scales of his hauberk.

"Dust that the wind blows away," mumbled the priest. "Sit down, Pyrrhas of Nippur, and let us converse with each other."

Pyrrhas glanced about the narrow chamber; at the even stacks of clay tablets along the walls, and the rolls of papyrus above them. Then he seated himself on the stone bench opposite the priest, hitching his sword-belt so that his hilt was well to the front.

"You are far from the cradle of your race," said Gimil-ishbi. "You are the first golden-haired rover to tread the plains of Shumir."

"I have wandered in many lands," muttered the

Argive, "but may the vultures pluck my bones if I ever saw a race so devil-ridden as this, or a land ruled and harried by so many gods and demons."

His gaze was fixed in fascination on Gimil-ishbi's hands; they were long, narrow, white and strong, the hands of youth. Their contrast to the priest's appearance of great age otherwise, was vaguely disquieting.

"To each city its gods and their priests," answered Gimil-ishbi; "and all fools. Of what account are gods whom the fortunes of men lift or lower? Behind all gods of men, behind the primal trinity of Ea, Anu and Enlil, lurk the elder gods, unchanged by the wars or ambitions of men. Men deny what they do not see. The priests of Eridu, which is sacred to Ea and light, are no blinder than them of Nippur, which is consecrated to Enlil, whom they deem the lord of Darkness. But he is only the god of the darkness of which men dream, not the real Darkness that lurks behind all dreams, and veils the real and awful deities. I glimpsed this truth when I was a priest of Enlil, wherefore they cast me forth. Ha! They would stare if they knew how many of their worshippers creep forth to me by night, as you have crept."

"I creep to no man!" the Argive bristled instantly. "I came to buy a charm. Name your price, and be damned to you."

"Be not wroth," smiled the priest. "Tell me why you have come."

"If you are so cursed wise you should know already," growled the Argive, unmollified. Then his gaze clouded as he cast back over his tangled trail.

"Some magician has cursed me," he muttered. "As I rode back from my triumph over Erech, my war-horse screamed and shied at Something none saw but he. Then my dreams grew strange and monstrous. In the darkness of my chamber, wings rustled and feet padded stealthily. Yesterday a woman at a feast went mad and tried to knife me. Later an adder sprang out of empty air and struck at me. Then, this night, she men call Lilitu came to my chamber and mocked me with awful laughter—"

"Lilitu?" the priest's eyes lit with a brooding fire; his skull-face worked in a ghastly smile. "Verily, warrior, they plot thy ruin in the House of Arabu. Your sword can not prevail against her, or against her mate Ardat Lili. In the gloom of midnight her teeth will find your throat. Her laugh will blast your ears, and her burning kisses will wither you like a dead leaf blowing in the hot winds of the desert. Madness and dissolution will be your lot, and you will descend to the House of Arabu whence none returns."

Pyrrhas moved restlessly, cursing incoherently beneath his breath.

"What can I offer you besides gold?" he growled.

"Much!" the black eyes shone; the mouth-gash twisted in inexplicable glee. "But I must name my own price, after I have given you aid."

Pyrrhas acquiesced with an impatient gesture.

"Who are the wisest men in the world?" asked the sage abruptly.

"The priests of Egypt, who scrawled on yonder parchments," answered the Argive.

Gimil-ishbi shook his head; his shadow fell on the wall like that of a great vulture, crouching over a dying victim.

"None so wise as the priests of Tiamat, who fools believe died long ago under the sword of Ea. Tiamat is deathless; she reigns in the shadows; she spread her dark wings over her worshippers."

"I know them not," muttered Pyrrhas uneasily.

"The cities of men know them not; but the waste-places know them, the reedy marshes, the stony deserts, the hills, and the caverns. To them steal the winged ones from the House of Arabu."

"I thought none came from that House," said the Argive.

"No *human* returns thence. But the servants of Tiamat come and go at their pleasure."

Pyrrhas was silent, reflecting on the place of the dead, as believed in by the Shumirians: a vast cavern, dusty, dark and silent, through which wandered the souls of the dead forever, shorn of all human attributes, cheerless and loveless, remembering their former lives only to hate all living men, their deeds and dreams.

"I will aid you," murmured the priest. Pyrrhas lifted his helmeted head and stared at him. Gimil-ishbi's eyes were no more human than the reflection of firelight on subterranean pools of inky blackness. His lips sucked in as if he gloated over all woes and miseries of mankind. Pyrrhas hated him as a man hates the unseen serpent in the darkness.

"Aid me and name your price," said the Argive.

Gimil-ishbi closed his hands and opened them, and in the palms lay a gold cask, the lid of which fastened with a jeweled catch. He sprung the lid, and Pyrrhas saw the cask was filled with grey dust. He shuddered without knowing why.

"This ground dust was once the skull of the first king of Ur," said Gimil-ishbi. "When he died, as even a necromancer must, he concealed his body with all his art. But I found his crumbling bones, and in the darkness above them, I fought with his soul as a man fights with a python in the night. My spoil was his skull, that held darker secrets than those that lie in the pits of Egypt.

"With this dead dust shall you trap Lilitu. Go quickly to an enclosed place—a cavern or a chamber—nay, that ruined villa which lies between this spot and the city will serve. Strew the dust in thin lines across threshold and window; leave not a spot as large as a man's hand unguarded. Then lie down as if in slumber. When Lilitu enters, as she will, speak the words I shall teach you. Then you are her master, until you free her again by repeating the conjure backwards. You can not slay her, but you can make her swear to leave you in peace. Make her swear by the dugs of Tiamat. Now lean close and I will whisper the words of the spell."

Somewhere in the night a nameless bird cried out harshly; the sound was more human than the whispering of the priest, which was no louder than the gliding of an adder through slimy ooze. He drew back, his gashmouth twisted in a grisly smile. The Argive sat for an instant like a statue of bronze. Their shadows fell together on the wall with the appearance of a crouching vulture facing a strange horned monster.

Pyrrhas took the cask and rose, wrapping his

crimson cloak about his somber figure, his horned helmet lending an illusion of abnormal height.

"And the price?"

Gimil-ishbi's hands became claws, quivering with lust.

"Blood! A life!"

"Whose life?"

"Any life! So blood flows, and there is fear and agony, a spirit ruptured from its quivering flesh! I have one price for all—a human life! Death is my rapture; I would glut my soul on death! Man, maid, or infant. You have sworn. Make good your oath! A life! A human life!"

"Aye, a life!" Pyrrhas' sword cut the air in a flaming arc and Gimil-ishbi's vulture head fell on the stone table. The body reared upright, spouting black blood, then slumped across the stone. The head rolled across the surface and thudded dully on the floor. The features stared up, frozen in a mask of awful surprise.

Outside there sounded a frightful scream as Pyrrhas' stallion broke its halter and raced madly away across the plain.

From the dim chamber with its tablets of cryptic cuneiforms and papyri of dark hieroglyphics, and from the remnants of the mysterious priest, Pyrrhas fled. As he climbed the carven stair and emerged into the starlight he doubted his own reason.

Far across the level plain the moon was rising, dull red, darkly lurid. Tense heat and silence held the land. Pyrrhas felt cold sweat thickly beading his flesh; his blood was a sluggish current of ice in his veins; his tongue clove to his palate. His

armor weighted him and his cloak was like a clinging snare. Cursing incoherently he tore it from
him; sweating and shaking he ripped off his armor,
piece by piece, and cast it away. In the grip of his
abysmal fears he had reverted to the primitive.
The veneer of civilization vanished. Naked but for
loin-cloth and girded sword he strode across the
plain, carrying the golden cask under his arm.

No sound disturbed the waiting silence as he
came to the ruined villa whose walls reared drunk-
enly among heaps of rubble. One chamber stood
above the general ruin, left practically untouched
by some whim of chance. Only the door had been
wrenched from its bronze hinges. Pyrrhas entered.
Moonlight followed him in and made a dim radiance inside the portal. There were three windows,
gold-barred. Sparingly he crossed the threshold
with a thin grey line. Each casement he served in
like manner. Then tossing aside the empty cask,
he stretched himself on a bare dais that stood in
deep shadow. His unreasoning horror was under
control. He who had been the hunted was now
the hunter. The trap was set, and he waited for
his prey with the patience of the primitive.

He had not long to wait. Something threshed
the air outside and the shadow of great wings
crossed the moon-lit portal. There was an instant
of tense silence in which Pyrrhas heard the thunderous impact of his own heart against his ribs.
Then a shadowy form framed itself in the open
door. A fleeting instant it was visible, then it vanished from view. The thing had entered; the night-
fiend was in the chamber.

Pyrrhas' hand clenched on his sword as he

heaved up suddenly from the dais. His voice crashed in the stillness as he thundered the dark enigmatic conjurement whispered to him by the dead priest. He was answered by a frightful scream; there was a quick stamp of bare feet, then a heavy fall, and something was threshing and writhing in the shadows on the floor. As Pyrrhas cursed the masking darkness, the moon thrust a crimson rim above the casement, like a goblin peering into a window, and a molten flood of light crossed the floor. In the pale glow the Argive saw his victim.

But it was no were-woman that writhed there. It was a thing like a man, lithe, naked, dusky-skinned. It differed not in the attributes of humanity except for the diquieting suppleness of its limbs, the changeless glitter of its eyes. It grovelled as in mortal agony, foaming at the mouth and contorting its body into impossible positions.

With a blood-mad yell Pyrrhas ran at the figure and plunged his sword through the squirming body. The point rang on the tiled floor beneath it, and an awful howl burst from the frothing lips, but that was the only apparent effect of the thrust. The Argive wrenched forth his sword and glared astoundedly to see no stain on the steel, no wound on the dusky body. He wheeled as the cry of the captive was re-echoed from without.

Just outside the enchanted threshold stood a woman, naked, supple, dusky, with wide eyes blazing in a soulless face. The being on the floor ceased to writhe, and Pyrrhas' blood turned to ice.

"Lilitu!"

She quivered at the threshold, as if held by an

invisible boundary. Her eyes were eloquent with hate, they yearned awfully for his blood and his life. She spoke, and the effect of a human voice issuing from that beautiful unhuman mouth was more terrifying than if a wild beast had spoken in human tongue.

"You have trapped my mate! You dare to torture Ardat Lili, before whom the gods tremble! Oh, you shall howl for this! You shall be torn bone from bone, and muscle from muscle, and vein from vein! Loose him! Speak the words and set him free, lest even this doom be denied you!"

"Words!" he answered with bitter savagery. "You have hunted me like a hound. Now you can not cross that line without falling into my hands as your mate has fallen. Come into the chamber, bitch of darkness, and let me caress you as I caress your lover—thus!—and thus!—and thus!"

Ardat Lili foamed and howled at the bite of the keen steel, and Lilitu screamed madly in protest, beating with her hands as at an invisible barrier.

"Cease! Cease! Oh, could I but come at you! How I would leave you a blind, mangled cripple! Have done! Ask what you will, and I will perform it!"

"That is well," grunted the Argive grimly. "I can not take this creature's life, but it seems I can hurt him, and unless you give me satisfaction, I will give him more pain than even he guesses exists in the world."

"Ask! Ask!" urged the were-woman, twisting with impatience.

"Why have you haunted me? What have I done to earn your hate?"

"Hate?" she tossed her head. "What are the sons of men that we of Shuala should hate or love? When the doom is loosed, it strikes blindly."

"Then who, or what, loosed the doom of Lilitu upon me?"

"One who dwells in the House of Arabu."

"Why, in Ymir's name?" swore Pyrrhas. "Why should the dead hate me?" He halted, remembering a priest who died gurgling curses.

"The dead strike at the bidding of the living. Someone who moves in the sunlight spoke in the night to one who dwells in Shuala."

"Who?"

"I do not know."

"You lie, you slut! It is the priests of Anu, and you would shield them. For that lie your lover shall howl to the kiss of the steel—"

"Butcher!" shrieked Lilitu. "Hold your hand! I swear by the dugs of Tiamat my mistress, I do not know what you ask. What are the priests of Anu that I should shield them? I would rip up all their bellies—as I would yours, could I come at you! Free my mate, and I will lead you to the House of Darkness itself, and you may wrest the truth from the awful mouth of the dweller himself, if you dare!"

"I will go," said Pyrrhas, "but I leave Ardat Lili here as hostage. If you deal falsely with me, he will writhe on this enchanted floor throughout all eternity.

Lilitu wept with fury, crying: "No devil in Shuala is crueller than you. Haste, in the name of Apsu!"

Sheathing his sword, Pyrrhas stepped across the

threshold. She caught his wrist with fingers like velvet-padded steel, crying something in a strange inhuman tongue. Instantly the moon-lit sky and plain were blotted out in a rush of icy blackness. There was a sensation of hurtling through a void intolerable coldness, a roaring in the Argive's ears as of titan winds. Then his feet struck solid ground; stability followed that chaotic instant, that had been like the instant of dissolution that joins or separates two states of being, alike in stability, but in kind more alien than day and night. Pyrrhas knew that in that instant he had crossed an unimaginable gulf, and that he stood on shores never before touched by living human feet.

Lilitu's fingers grasped his wrist, but he could not see her. He stood in darkness of a quality which he had never encountered. It was almost tangibly soft, all-pervading and all-engulfing. Standing amidst it, it was not easy even to imagine sunlight and bright rivers and grass singing in the wind. They belonged to that other world—a world lost and forgotten in the dust of a million centuries. The world of life and light was a whim of chance—a bright spark glowing momentarily in a universe of dust and shadows. Darkness and silence were the natural state of the cosmos, not light and the noises of Life. No wonder the dead hated the living, who disturbed the grey stillness of Infinity with their tinkling laughter.

Lilitu's fingers drew him through abysmal blackness. He had a vague sensation as of being in a titanic cavern, too huge for conception. He sensed walls and roof, though he did not see them and never reached them; they seemed to recede as he advanced, yet there was always the sensation of their presence. Sometimes his feet stirred what he hoped was only dust. There was a dusty scent throughout the darkness; he smelled the odors of decay and mould.

He saw lights moving like glow-worms through the dark. Yet they were not lights, as he knew radiance. They were more like spots of lesser gloom, that seemed to glow only by contrast with the engulfing blackness which they emphasized without illuminating. Slowly, laboriously they crawled through the eternal night. One approached the companions closely and Pyrrhas' hair stood up and he grasped his sword. But Lilitu took no heed as she hurried him on. The dim spot glowed close to him for an instant; it vaguely illumined a shadowy countenance, faintly human, yet strangely birdlike.

Existence became a dim and tangled thing to Pyrrhas, wherein he seemed to journey for a thousand years through the blackness of dust and decay, drawn and guided by the hand of the werewoman. Then he heard her breath hiss through her teeth, and she came to a halt.

Before them shimmered another of those strange globes of light. Pyrrhas could not tell whether it illumined a man or a bird. The creature stood upright like a man, but it was clad in grey feathers—at least they were more like feathers than anything else. The features were no more human than they were birdlike.

"This is the dweller in Shuala which put upon you the curse of the dead," whispered Lilitu. "Ask him the name of him who hates you on earth."

"Tell me the name of mine enemy!" demanded Pyrrhas, shuddering at the sound of his own voice, which whispered drearily and uncannily through the unechoing darkness.

The eyes of the dead burned redly and it came at him with a rustle of pinions, a long gleam of light springing into its lifted hand. Pyrrhas recoiled, clutching at his sword, but Lilitu hissed: "Nay, use this!" and he felt a hilt thrust into his fingers. He was grasping a scimitar with a blade curved in the shape of the crescent moon, that shone like an arc of white fire.

He parried the bird-thing's stroke, and sparks showered in the gloom, burning him like bits of flame. The darkness clung to him like a black cloak; the glow of the feathered monster bewildered and baffled him. It was like fighting a shadow in the maze of a nightmare. Only by the fiery gleam of his enemy's blade did he keep the touch of it. Thrice it sang death in his ears as he deflected it by the merest fraction, then his own crescent-edge cut the darkness and grated on the other's shoulder-joint. With a strident screech the thing dropped its weapon and slumped down, a milky liquid spurting from the gaping wound. Pyrrhas lifted his scimitar again, when the creature gasped in a voice that was no more human than the grating of wind-blown boughs against one another: "Naram-ninub, the great-grandson of my great-grandson! By black arts he spoke and commanded me across the gulfs!"

"Naram-ninub!" Pyrrhas stood frozen in amazement; the scimitar was torn from his hand. Again Lilitu's fingers locked on his wrist. Again the dark was drowned in deeper blackness and howling winds blowing between the spheres.

He staggered in the moonlight without the ruined villa, reeling with the dizziness of his transmutation. Beside him Lilitu's teeth shone between her curling red lips. Catching the thick locks clustered on her neck, he shook her savagely, as he would have shaken a mortal woman.

"Harlot of Hell! What madness has your sorcery instilled in my brain?"

"No madness!" she laughed, striking his hand aside. "You have journeyed to the House of Arabu, and you have returned. You have spoken with and overcome with the sword of Apsu, the shade of a man dead for long centuries."

"Then it was no dream of madness! But Naram-ninub—" he halted in confused thought. "Why, of all the men of Nippur, he has been my staunchest friend!"

"Friend?" she mocked. "What is friendship but a pleasant pretense to while away an idle hour?"

"But why, in Ymir's name?"

"What are the petty intrigues of men to me?" she exclaimed angrily. "Yet now I remember that men from Erech, wrapped in cloaks, steal by night to Naram-ninub's palace."

"Ymir!" like a sudden blaze of light Pyrrhas saw reason in merciless clarity. "He would sell Nippur to Erech, and first he must put me out of the way, because the hosts of Nippur cannot stand before me! Oh, dog, let my knife find your heart!"

"Keep faith with me!" Lilitu's importunities drowned his fury. "I have kept faith with you. I have led you where never living man has trod, and brought you forth unharmed. I have betrayed the dwellers in darkness and done that for which Tiamat will bind me naked on a white-hot grid for seven times seven days. Speak the words and free Ardat Lili!"

Still engrossed in Naram-ninub's treachery, Pyrrhas spoke the incantation. With a loud sigh of relief, the were-man rose from the tiled floor and came into the moonlight. The Argive stood with his hand on his sword and his head bent, lost in moody thought. Lilitu's eyes flashed a quick meaning to her mate. Lithely they began to steal toward the abstracted man. Some primitive instinct brought his head up with a jerk. They were closing in on him, their eyes burning in the moonlight, their fingers reaching for him. Instantly he realized his mistake; he had forgotten to make them swear truce with him; no oath bound them from his flesh.

With feline screeches they struck in, but quicker yet he bounded aside and raced toward the distant city. Too hotly eager for his blood to resort to sorcery, they gave chase. Fear winged his feet, but close behind him he heard the swift patter of their feet, their eager panting. A sudden drum of hoofs sounded in front of him, and burst through a tattered grove of skeleton palms, he almost caromed against a rider, who rode like the wind, a long silvery glitter in his hand. With a startled oath the horseman wrenched his steed back on its haunches. Pyrrhas saw looming over him a powerful body in scale-mail, a pair of blazing eyes that glared at him from under a domed helmet, a short black beard.

"You dog!" he yelled furiously. "Damn you, have you come to complete with your sword what your black magic began?"

The steed reared wildly as he leaped at its head and caught its bridle. Cursing madly and fighting for balance, Naram-ninub slashed at his attacker's head, but Pyrrhas parried the stroke and thrust upward murderously. The sword-point glanced from the corselet and plowed along the Semite's jaw-bone. Naram-ninub screamed and fell from the plunging steed, spouting blood. His leg-bone snapped as he pitched heavily to earth, and his cry was echoed by a gloating howl from the shadowed grove.

Without dragging the rearing horse to earth, Pyrrhas sprang to its back and wrenched it about. Naram-ninub was groaning and writhing on the ground, and as Pyrrhas looked, two shadows darted from the darkened grove and fastened themselves on his prostrate form. A terrible scream burst from his lips, echoed by more awful laughter. Blood on the night air; on it the night-things would feed, wild as mad dogs, making no difference between men.

The Argive wheeled away, toward the city, then hesitated, shaken by a fierce revulsion. The level land lay quiescent beneath the moon, and the brutish pyramid of Enlil stood up in the stars. Behind him lay his enemy, glutting the fangs of the horrors he himself had called up from the Pits. The road was open to Nippur, for his return.

His return?—to a devil-ridden people crawling beneath the heels of priest and king; to a city rotten with intrigue and obscene mysteries; to an alien race that mistrusted him, and a mistress that hated him.

Wheeling his horse again, he rode westward toward the open lands, flinging his arms wide in a gesture of renunciation and the exultation of freedom. The weariness of life dropped from him like a cloak. His mane floated in the wind, and over the plains of Shumir shouted a sound they had never heard before—the gutsy, elemental, reasonless laughter of a free barbarian.

Howard's imagination drew on history but refused to be confined by it—he was a fantasist, after all. Here we have two refugees from what were probably intended to be a tribe of proto-Aryans, despite their Germanic names, which would in truth probably have been polysyllabic and full of consonants. Ironically enough, recent investigation of the mummies found in the wastes of the Tarim Basin in far western China indicate that Howard was probably right about the physical appearance of the earliest Indo-Europeans; they really were tall and blond, although in Howard's day this was pure speculation fueled by racist myth. Besides the ur-Nordic wanderers, in the Garden of Fear we have two more of his favorite themes; the last, degenerate survivor of an evil race, and a horde of carnivorous bloodsucking plants. Perhaps the ubiquitous kudzu of the South finds a literary apothesis here. . .

THE GARDEN OF FEAR

Once I was Hunwulf, the Wanderer. I cannot explain my knowledge of this fact by any occult or esoteric means, not shall I try. A man remembers his past life; I remember my past *lives*. Just as a normal individual recalls the shapes that were him in childhood, boyhood and youth, so I recall the shapes that have been James Allison is forgotten ages. Why this memory is mine I cannot say, any more than I can explain the myriad other phenomena of nature which daily confront me and every other mortal. But as I lie waiting for death to free me from my long disease. I see with a clear, sure sight the grand panorama of lives that trail out behind me. I see the men who have been me, and I see the beasts that have been me.

For my memory does not end at the coming of Man. How could it, when the beast so shades into Man that there is no clearly divided line to mark the boundaries of bestiality? At this instant I see a dim twilight vista, among the gigantic trees of primordial forest that never knew the tread of a leather-shod foot. I see a vast, shaggy, shambling bulk that lumbers clumsily yet swiftly, sometimes upright, sometimes on all fours. He delves under rotten logs for grubs and insects, and his small ears twitch continually. He lifts his head and bares yellow fangs. He is primordial, bestial, anthropoid; yet I recognize his kinship with the entity now called James Allison. Kinship? Say rather oneness, I am he; he is I. My flesh is soft and white and hairless; his is dark and tough and shaggy. Yet we were one, and already in his feeble, shadowed brain are beginning to stir and tingle the man-thoughts and the man dreams, crude, chaotic, fleeting, yet the basis for all the high and lofty visions men have dreamed in all the following ages.

Nor does my knowledge cease there. It goes back, back, down immemorial vistas I dare not follow, to abysses too dark and awful for the human mind to plumb. Yet even there I am aware of my identity, my individuality. I tell you the individual is never lost, neither in the black pit from which we once crawled, blind, squalling and noisome, or in that eventual Nirvana in which we shall one day sink—which I have glimpsed afar off, shining as a blue twilight lake among the mountains of the stars.

But enough. I would tell you of Hunwulf. Oh, it was long, long ago! How long ago I dare not say. Why should I seek for paltry human comparisons to describe a realm indescribably, incomprehensibly distant? Since that age the earth had altered her contours not once but a dozen times, and whole cycles of mankind have completed their destinies.

I was Hunwulf, a son of the golden-haired Aesir, who, from the icy plains of shadowy Asgard, sent blue-eyed tribes around the world in century-long drifts to leave their trails in strange places. On one of those southward drifts I was born, for I never saw the homeland of my people, where the bulk of the Nordheimer still dwelt in their horse-hide tents among the snows.

I grew to manhood on that long wandering, to the fierce, sinewy, untamed manhood of the Aesir, who knew no gods but Ymir of the frost-rimmed beard, and whose axes are stained with the blood of many nations. My thews were like woven steel cords. My yellow hair fell in a lion-like mane to my mighty shoulders. My loins were girt with leopard skin. With either hand I could wield my heavy flint-headed axe.

Year by year my tribe drifted southward, sometimes swinging in long arcs to east or west, sometimes lingering for months or years in fertile valleys or plains where the grass-eaters swarmed, but always forging slowly and inevitably southward. Sometimes our way led through vast and breathless solitudes that had never known a human cry; sometimes strange tribes disputed our course, and our trail passed over bloodstained ashes of butchered villages. And amidst this wandering, hunting and slaughtering, I came to full manhood and the love of Gudrun.

What shall I say of Gudrun? How describe color to the blind? I can say that her skin was whiter than milk, that her hair was living gold with the flame of sun caught in it, that the supple beauty of her body would shame the dream that shaped the Grecian goddesses. But I cannot make you realize the fire and wonder that was Gudrun. You have no basis for comparison; you know womanhood only by the women of your epoch, who, beside her are like candles beside the glow of the full moon. Not for a millennium of millenniums have women like Gudrun walked the earth. Cleopatra, Thais, Helen of Troy, they were but pallid shadows of her beauty, frail mimicries of the blossom that blooms to full glory only in the primordial.

For Gudrun I forsook my tribe and my people, and went into the wilderness, an exile and an outcast, with blood on my hands. She was of my race, but not of my tribe: a waif whom we found as a child wandering in a dark forest, lost from some wandering tribe of our blood. She grew up in the tribe, and when she came to the full ripeness of her glorious young womanhood, she was given to Heimdul the Strong, the mightiest hunter of the tribe.

But the dream of Gudrun was madness in my soul, a flame that burned eternally, and for her I slew Heimdul, crushing his skull with my flint-headed axe ere he could bear her to his horse-hide tent. And then follows our long flight from the vengeance of the tribe. Willingly she went with me, for she loved me with the love of the Aesir women, which is a devouring flame that destroys weakness. Oh, it was a savage age, when life was grim and bloodstained, and the weak died quickly. There was nothing mild or gentle about us; our passions were those of the tempest, the surge and impact of battle, the challenge of the lion. Our loves were as terrible as our hates.

And so I carried Gudrun from the tribe, and the killers were hot on our trail. For a night and a day they pressed us hard, until we swam a rising river, a roaring, foaming torrent that even the men of the Aesir dared not attempt. But in the madness of our love and recklessness we buffetted our way across, beaten and torn by the frenzy of the flood, and reached the farther bank alive.

Then for many days we traversed upland forests haunted by tigers and leopards, until we came to a great barrier of mountains, blue ramparts climbing awesomely to the sky. Slope piled upon slope.

In those mountains we were assailed by freezing winds and hunger, and by giant condors which swept down upon us with a thunder of gigantic wings. In grim battles in the passes I shot away all my arrows and splintered my flintheaded spear, but at last we crossed the bleak backbone of the range and descending the southern slopes, came upon a village of mud huts among the cliffs inhabited by a peaceful, brown-skinned people who spoke a strange tongue and had strange customs. But they greeted us with the sign of peace, and brought us into their village, where they set meat and barley-bread and fermented milk before us, and squatted in a ring about us while we ate, and a woman slapped softly on a bowl-shaped tom-tom to do us honor.

We had reached their village at dusk, and night fell while we feasted. On all sides rose the cliffs and peaks smouldering massively against the stars. The little cluster of mud huts and the tiny fires were drowned and lost in the immensity of the night. Gudrun felt the loneliness, the crowding desolation of that darkness, and she pressed close to me, her shoulder against my breast. But my ax was close at my hand, and I had never known the sensation of fear.

The little brown people squatted before us, men and women, and tried to talk to us with motions of their slender hands. Dwelling always in one place, in comparative security, they lacked both the strength and the uncompromising ferocity of the nomadic Aesir. Their hands fluttered with friendly gestures in the firelight.

I made them understand that we had come from the north, had crossed the backbone of the great mountain range, and that on the morrow it was our intention to descend into the green tablelands which we had glimpsed southward of the peaks.

When they understood my meaning they set up a great cry shaking their heads violently, and beating madly on the drum. They were all so eager to impart something to me, and all waving their hands at once, that they bewildered rather than enlightened me. Eventually they did make me understand that they did not wish me to descend the mountains. Some menace lay to the south of the village, but whether of man or beast, I could not learn.

It was while they were all gesticulating and my whole attention was centered on their gestures, that the blow fell. The first intimation was a sudden thunder of wings in my ears; a dark shape rushed out of the night, and a great pinion dealt me a buffet over the head as I turned. I was knocked sprawling, and in that instant I heard Gudrun scream as she was torn from my side. Bounding up, quivering with a furious eagerness to rend and slay, I saw the dark shape vanish again into the darkness, a white, screaming, writhing figure trailing from its talons.

Roaring my grief and fury I caught up my ax and charged into the dark—then halted short, wild, desperate, knowing not which way to turn.

The little brown people had scattered, screaming, knocking sparks from their fires as they rushed over them in their haste to gain their huts, but now they crept out fearfully, whimpering like wounded dogs. They gathered around me and plucked at me with timid hands and chattered in their tongue while I cursed in sick impotency, knowing they wished to tell me something which I could not understand.

At last I suffered them to lead me back to the fire, and there the oldest man of the tribe brought forth a strip of cured hide, a clay pot of pigments, and a stick. On the hide he painted a crude picture of a winged thing carrying a white woman—oh, it was very crude, but I made out his meaning. Then all pointed southward and cried out loudly in their own tongue; and I knew that the menace they had warned me against was the thing that had carried off Gudrun. Until then I supposed that it had been one of the great mountain condors which had carried her away, but the picture the old man drew, in black paint, resembled a winging man more than anything else.

Then, slowly and laboriously, he began to trace something I finally recognized as a map—oh, yes, even in those dim days we had our primitive maps, though no modern man would be able to comprehend them so greatly different was our symbolism.

It took a long time; it was midnight before the old man had finished and I understood his tracings. But at last the matter was made clear. If I followed the course traced on the map, down the long narrow valley where stood the village, across a plateau, down a series of rugged slopes and along another valley, I would come to the place where lurked the being which had stolen my woman. At that spot the old man drew what looked like a misshapen hut, with many strange markings all about it in red pigments. Pointing to these, and again to me, he shook his head, with those loud cries that seemed to indicate peril among these people.

Then they tried to persuade me not to go, but afire with eagerness I took the piece of hide and pouch of food they thrust into my hands (they were indeed a strange people for that age), grasped my ax and set off in the moonless darkness. But my eyes were keener than a modern mind can comprehend, and my sense of direction was as a wolf's. Once the map was fixed in my mind, I could have thrown it away and come unerring to the place I sought but I folded it and thrust it into my girdle.

I traveled at my best speed through the starlight, taking no heed of any beasts that might be seeking their prey—cave bear or saber-toothed tiger. At times I heard gravel slide under stealthy padded paws; I glimpsed fierce yellow eyes burning in the darkness, and caught sight of shadowy, skulking forms. But I plunged on recklessly, in too desperate a mood to give the path to any beast however fearsome.

I traversed the valley, climbed a ridge and came out on a broad plateau, gashed with ravines and strown with boulders. I crossed this and in the darkness before dawn commenced my climb down the treacherous slopes. They seemed endless, falling away in a long steep incline until their feet were lost in darkness. But I went down recklessly, not pausing to unsling the rawhide rope I carried about my shoulders, trusting to my luck and skill to bring me down without a broken neck.

And just as dawn was touching the peaks with a white glow, I dropped into a broad valley, walled by stupendous cliffs. At that point it was wide from east to west, but the cliffs converged toward the lower end, giving the valley the appearance of a great fan, narrowing swiftly toward the south.

The floor was level, traversed by a winding stream. Trees grew thinly; there was no underbrush, but a carpet of tall grass, which at that time of year were somewhat dry. Along the stream where the green lush grew, wandered mammoths, hairy mountains of flesh and muscle.

I gave them a wide berth, giants too mighty for me to cope with, confident in their power, and afraid of only one thing on earth. They bent forward their great ears and lifted their trunks menacingly when I approached too near, but they did not attack me. I ran swiftly among the trees, and the sun was not yet above the eastern ramparts which its rising edged with golden flame, when I came to the point where the cliffs converged. My night-long climb had not affected my iron muscles. I felt no weariness; my fury burned unabated. What lay beyond the cliffs I could not know; I ventured no conjecture. I had room in my brain only for red wrath and killing-lust.

The cliffs did not form a solid wall. That is, the extremities of the converging palisades did not meet, leaving a notch or gap a few hundred feet wide, and emerged into a second valley, or rather into a continuance of the same valley which broadened out again beyond the pass.

The cliffs slanted away swiftly to east and west, to form a giant rampart that marched clear around the valley in the shape of a vast oval. It formed a blue rim all around the valley without a break except for a glimpse of the clear sky that seemed to mark another notch at the southern end. The inner valley was shaped much like a great bottle, with two necks.

The neck by which I entered was crowded with trees, which grew densely for several hundred yards, when they gave way abruptly to a field of crimson flowers. And a few hundred yards beyond the edges of the trees, I saw a strange structure.

I must speak of what I saw not alone as Hunwulf, but as James Allison as well. For Hunwulf only vaguely comprehended the things he saw, and, as Hunwulf, he could not describe them at all. I, as Hunwulf, knew nothing of architecture. The only man-built dwelling I had ever seen had been the horse-hide tents of my people, and the thatched mud huts of the barley people—and other people equally primitive.

So as Hunwulf I could only say that I looked upon a great hut the construction of which was beyond my comprehension. But I, James Allison, know that it was a tower, some seventy feet in height, of a curious green stone, highly polished, and of a substance that created the illusion of semi-translucency. It was cylindrical, and, as near as I could see, without doors or windows. The main body of the building was perhaps sixty feet in height, and from its center rose a smaller tower that completed its full stature. This tower, being much inferior in girth to the main body of the structure, and thus surrounded by a sort of gallery, with a crenellated parapet, and was furnished with both doors, curiously arched, and windows, thickly barred as I could see, even from where I stood.

That was all. No evidence of human occupancy. No sign of life in all the valley. But it was evident that this castle was what the old man of the mountain village had been trying to draw; and I was certain that in it I would find Gudrun—if she still lived.

Beyond the tower I saw the glimmer of a blue lake into which the stream, following the curve of the western wall, eventually flowed. Lurking amid the trees I glared at the tower and at the flowers surrounding it on all sides, growing thick along the walls and extending for hundreds of yards in all directions. There were trees at the other end of the valley, near the lake; but no trees grew among the flowers.

They were not like any plants I had ever seen. They grew close together, almost touching each other. They were some four feet in height, with only one blossom on each stalk, a blossom larger than a man's head, with broad, fleshy petals drawn close together. These petals were a livid crimson, the hue of an open wound. The stalks were thick as a man's wrist, colorless, almost transparent. The poisonously green leaves were shaped like spearheads, drooping on long snaky stems. Their whole aspect was repellent, and I wondered what their denseness concealed.

For all my wild-born instincts were roused in me. I felt lurking peril, just as I had often sensed the ambushed lion before my external senses recognized him. I scanned the dense blossoms closely, wondering if some great serpent lay coiled among them. My nostrils expanded as I quested for a scent, but the wind was blowing away from me. But there was something decidedly unnatural about that vast garden. Though the north wind swept over it, not a blossom stirred, not a leaf rustled; they hung motionless, sullen, like birds of prey with drooping heads, and I had a strange feeling that they were watching me like living things.

It was like a landscape in a dream: on either hand the blue cliffs lifting against the cloud-fleeced sky; in the distance the dreaming lake; and that fantastic green tower rising in the midst of that livid crimson field.

And there was something else: in spite of the wind that was blowing away from me, I caught a scent, a charnel-house reek of death and decay and corruption that rose from the blossoms.

Then suddenly I crouched closer in my covert. There was life and movement on the castle. A figure emerged from the tower, and coming to the parapet, leaned upon it and looked out across the valley. It was a man, but such a man as I had never dreamed of, even in nightmares.

He was tall, powerful, black with the hue of polished ebony; but the feature which made a human nightmare of him was the batlike wings which folded on his shoulders. I knew they were wings: the fact was obvious and indisputable.

I, James Allison, have pondered much on that phenomenon which I have witnessed through the eyes of Hunwulf. Was that winged man merely a freak, an isolated example of distorted nature, dwelling in solitude and immemorial desolation? Or was he a survival of a forgotten race, which had risen, reigned and vanished before the coming of man as we know him? The little brown people of the hills might have told me, but we had no speech in common. Yet I am inclined to the latter theory. Winged men are not uncommon in mythology;

they are met with in the folk lore of many nations and many races. As far back as man may go in myth, chronicle and legend, he finds tales of harpies and winged gods, angels and demons. Legends are distorted shadows of pre-existent realities. I believe that once a race of winged black men ruled a pre-Adamite world, and that I, Hunwulf, met the last survivor of that race in the valley of the red blossoms.

These thoughts I think as James Allison, with my modern knowledge which is as imponderable as my modern ignorance.

I, Hunwulf, indulged in no such speculations. Modern skepticism was not a part of my nature, nor did I seek to rationalize what seemed not to coincide with a natural universe. I acknowledged no gods but Ymir and his daughters, but I did not doubt the existence—as demons—of other deities, worshipped by other races. Supernatural beings of all sorts fitted into my conception of life and the universe. I no more doubted the existence of dragons, ghosts, fiends and devils than I doubted the existence of loins and buffaloes and elephants. I accepted this freak of nature as a supernatural demon and did not worry about its origin or source. Nor was I thrown into a panic of superstitious fear. I was a son of Asgard, who feared neither man nor devil, and I had more faith in the crushing power of my flint axe than in the spells of priests or the incantations of sorcerers.

But I did not immediately rush into the open and charge the tower. The wariness of the wild was mine, and I saw no way to climb the castle. The winged man needed no doors on the side, because he evidently entered at the top, and the slick surface of the walls seemed to defy the most skillful climber. Presently a way of getting upon the tower occurred to me, but I hesitated, waiting to see if any other winged people appeared, though I had an unexplainable feeling that he was the only one of his kind in the valley—possibly in the world. While I crouched among the trees and watched, I saw him lift his elbows from the parapet and stretch lithely, like a great cat. Then he strode across the circular gallery and entered the tower. A muffled cry rang out on the air which caused me to stiffen, though even so I realized that it was not the cry of a woman. Presently the black master of the castle emerged, dragging a smaller figure with him—a figure which writhed and struggled and cried out piteously. I saw that it was a small brown man, much like those of the mountain village. Captured, I did not doubt, as Gudrun had been captured.

He was like a child in the hands of his huge foe. The black man spread broad wings and rose over the parapet, carrying his captive as a condor might carry a sparrow. He soared out over the field of blossoms, while I crouched in my leafy retreat, glaring in amazement.

The winged man, hovering in mid-air, voiced a strange weird cry; and it was answered in horrible fashion. A shudder of awful life passed over the crimson field beneath him. The great red blossoms trembled, opened, spreading their fleshy petals like the mouths of serpents. Their stalk seemed to elongate, stretching upward eagerly. Their broad leaves lifted and vibrated with a curious lethal whirring, like the singing of a rattlesnake. A faint but flesh-crawling hissing sounded over all the valley. The blossoms gasped, straining upward. And with a fiendish laugh, the winged man dropped his writhing captive.

With a scream of a lost soul the brown man hurtled downward, crashing among the flowers. And with a rustling hiss, they were on him. Their thick flexible stalks arched like the necks of serpents, their petals closed on his flesh. A hundred blossoms clung to him like the tentacles of an octopus, smothering and crushing him down. His shrieks of agony came muffled; he was completely hidden by the hissing, threshing flowers. Those beyond reach swayed and writhed furiously as if seeking to tear up their roots in their eagerness to join their brothers. All over the field the great red blossoms leaned and strained toward the spot where the grisly battle went on. The shrieks sank lower and lower and lower, and ceased. A dread silence reigned over the valley. The black man flapped his way leisurely back to the tower, and vanished within it.

Then presently the blossoms detached themselves one by one from their victim who lay very white and still. Aye, his whiteness was more than that of death; he was like a wax image, a staring effigy from which every drop of blood had been sucked. And a startling transmutation was evident in the flowers directly about him. Their stalks no longer colorless; they were swollen and dark red, like transparent bamboos filled to the bursting with fresh blood.

Drawn by an insatiable curiosity, I stole from

the trees and glided to the very edge of the red field. The blossoms hissed and bent toward me, spreading their petals like the hood of a roused cobra. Selecting one farthest from its brothers, I severed the stalk with a stroke of my axe, and the thing tumbled to the ground, writhing like a beheaded serpent.

When its struggles ceased I bent over it in wonder. The stalk was not hollow, as I had supposed—that is, hollow like a dry bamboo. It was traversed by a network of thread-like veins, some empty and some exuding a colorless sap. The stems which held the leaves to the stalk were remarkably tenacious and pliant, and the leaves themselves were edged with curved spines, like sharp hooks.

Once those spines were sunk in the flesh, the victim would be forced to tear up the whole plant by the roots if he escaped.

The petals were each as broad as my hand, and as thick as a prickly pear, and on the inner side covered with innumerable tiny mouths, not larger than the head of a pin. In the center, where the pistil should be, there was a barbed spike, of a substance like thorn, and narrow channels between the four serrated edges.

From my investigations of this horrible travesty of vegetation, I looked up suddenly, just in time to see the winged man appear again on the parapet. He did not seem particularly surprised to see me. He shouted in his unknown tongue and made a mocking gesture, while I stood statue-like, gripping my axe. Presently he turned and entered the tower as he had done before; and as before, he emerged with a captive. My fury and hate were almost submerged by the flood of joy that Gudrun was alive.

In spite of her supple strength, which was that of a she-panther, the black man handled Gudrun as easily as he had handled the brown man. Lifting her struggling white body high above his head, he displayed her to me and yelled tauntingly. Her golden hair streamed over her white shoulders as she fought vainly, crying to me in the terrible extremity of her fright and horror. Not lightly was a woman of the Aesir reduced to cringing terror. I measured the depths of her captor's diabolism by her frenzied cries.

But I stood motionless. If it would have saved her, I would have plunged into that crimson morass of hell, to be hooked and pierced and sucked white by those fiendish flowers. But that would help her none. My death would merely leave her without a defender. So I stood silent while she writhed and whimpered, and the black man's laughter sent red waves of madness surging across my brain. Once he made as if to cast her down among the flowers, and my iron control almost snapped and sent me plunging into that red sea of hell. But it was only a gesture. Presently he dragged her back to the tower and tossed her inside. Then he turned back to the parapet, rested his elbows upon it, and fell to watching me. Apparently he was playing with us as a cat plays with a mouse before he destroys it.

But while he watched, I turned my back and strode into the forest. I, Hunwulf, was not a thinker, as modern men understand the term. I lived in an age where emotions were translated by the smash of a flint axe rather than by emanations of the intellect. Yet I was not the senseless animal the black man evidently supposed me to be. I had a human brain, whetted by the eternal struggle for existence and supremacy.

I knew I could not cross that red strip that banded the castle, alive. Before I could take a half dozen steps a score of barbed spikes would be thrust into my flesh, their avid mouths sucking the flood from my veins to feed their demoniac lust. Even my tigerish strength would not avail to hew a path through them.

The winged man did not follow. Looking back, I saw him still lounging in the same position. When I, as James Allison, dream again the dreams of Hunwulf, that image is etched in my mind, that gargoyle figure with elbows propped on the parapet, like medieval devil brooding on the battlements of hell.

I passed through the straits of the valley and came into the vale beyond where the trees thinned and the mammoths lumbered along the stream. Beyond the herd I stopped and drawing a pair of flints into my pouch, stooped and struck a spark in the dry grass. Running swiftly from chosen place to place, I set a dozen fires, in a great semi-circle. The north wind caught them, whipped them into eager life, drove them before it. In a few moments a rampart of flame was sweeping down the valley.

The mammoths ceased their feeding, lifted their great ears and bellowed alarm. In all the world they feared only fire. They began to retreat southward, the cows herding the calves before them, bulls trumpeting like the blast of Judgement Day.

Roaring like a storm the fire rushed on, and the mammoths broke and stampeded, a crushing hurricane of flesh, a thundering earthquake of hurtling bone and muscle. Trees splintered and went down before them, the ground shook under their headlong tread. Behind them came the racing fire and on the heels of the fire came I, so closely that the smouldering earth burnt the moose-hide sandals off my feet.

Through the narrow neck they thundered, levelling the dense thickets like a giant scythe. Trees were torn up by the roots; it was as if a tornado had ripped through the pass.

With a deafening thunder of pounding feet and trumpeting, they stormed across the sea of red blossoms. Those devilish plants might have even pulled down and destroyed a single mammoth; but under the impact of the whole herd, they were no more than common flowers. The maddened titans crashed through and over them, battering them to shreds, hammering, stamping them into the earth which grew soggy with their juice.

I trembled for an instant, fearing the brutes would not turn aside for the castle, and dubious of even it being able to withstand that battering ram concussion. Evidently the winged man shared my fears, for he shot up from the tower and raced off through the sky toward the lake. But one of the bulls butted head-on into the wall, was shunted off the smooth curving surface, caromed into the one next to him, and the herd split and roared by the tower on either hand, so closely their hairy sides rasped against it. They thundered on through the red field toward the distant lake.

The fire, reaching the edge of the trees, was checked; the smashed sappy fragments of the red flowers would not burn. Trees, fallen or standing, smoked and burst into flame, and burning branches showered around me as I ran through the trees and out into the gigantic swath the charging herd had cut through the livid field.

As I ran I shouted to Gudrun and she answered me. Her voice was muffled and accompanied by a hammering on something. The winged man had locked her in a tower.

As I came under the castle wall, treading on remnants of red petals and snaky stalks, I unwound my rawhide rope, swung it, and sent its loop shooting upward to catch on one of the merlons of the crenellated parapet. Then I went up it, hand over hand, gripping the rope between my toes, bruising my knuckles and elbows against the sheer wall as I swung about.

I was within five feet of the parapet when I was galvanized by the beat of wings about my head. The black man shot out of the air and landed on the gallery. I got a good look at him as he leaned over the parapet. His features were straight and regular; there was no suggestion of the negroid about him. His eyes were slanted slits, and his teeth gleamed in a savage grin of hate and triumph. Long, long he had ruled the valley of the red blossoms, levelling tribute of human lives from the miserable tribes of the hills, for writhing victims to feed the carnivorous half-bestial flowers which were his subjects and protectors. And now I was in his power, my fierceness, and craft gone for naught. A stroke of the crooked dagger in his hand and I would go hurtling to my death. Somewhere Gudrun, seeing my peril, was screaming like a wild thing, and then a door crashed with a splintering of wood.

The black man, intent upon his gloating, laid the keen edge of his dagger on the rawhide strand—then a strong white arm locked about his neck from behind, and he was jerked violently backward. Over his shoulder I saw the beautiful face of Gudrun, her hair standing on end, her eyes dilated with terror and fury.

With a roar he turned in her grasp, tore loose her clinging arms and hurled her against the tower with such force that she lay half stunned. Then he turned again to me, but in that instant I had swarmed up and over the parapet, and leaped upon the gallery, unslinging my ax.

For an instant he hesitated, his wings half-lifted, his hand poising on his dagger, as if uncertain whether to fight or take to the air. He was a giant in stature, with muscles standing out in corded ridges all over him, but he hesitated, as uncertain as a man when confronted by a wild beast.

I did not hesitate. With a deep-throated roar I sprang, swinging my ax with all my giant strength. With a strangled cry he threw up his arms; but down between them the ax plunged and blasted his head to red ruin.

I wheeled toward Gudrun; and struggling to her knees, she threw her white arms about me in a desperate clasp of love and terror, staring awedly to where lay the winged lord of the valley, the crimson pulp that had been his head drowned in a puddle of blood and brains.

I had often wished that it were possible to draw these various lives of mine together in one body, combining the experiences of Hunwulf and the knowledge of James Allison. Could that be so, Hunwulf would have gone through the ebony door which Gudrun in her desperate strength had shattered, into that weird chamber he glimpsed through the ruined panels, with fantastic furnishing, and shelves heaped with rolls of parchment. He would have unrolled those scrolls and pored over their characters until he deciphered them, and read, perhaps, the chronicles of that weird race whose last survivor he had just slain. Surely the tale was stranger than an opium dream, and marvelous as the story of lost Atlantis.

But Hunwulf had no such curiosity. To him the tower, the ebony furnished chamber and the rolls of parchment were meaningless, inexplicable emanations of sorcery, whose significance lay only in their diabolism. Though the solution of mystery lay under his fingers, he was a far removed from it as James Allison, millenniums yet unborn.

To me, Hunwulf, the castle was but a monstrous trap, concerning which I had but one emotion, and that a desire to escape from it as quickly as possible.

With Gudrun clinging to me I slid to the ground, then with a dextrous flip I freed my rope and wound it; and after that we went hand and hand along the path made by the mammoths, now vanishing in the distance, toward the blue lake at the southern end of the valley and the notch in the cliffs beyond it.

"Celt" is among the most ambiguous terms in European ethnology. Howard knew what he meant by it, however—to him it meant the wild spirit of the fighting Gaels of old, whom he was proud to count among his ancestors; and whose fickleness, facetiousness, and chaotic individualism he also acknowledged and celebrated. Ancient Ireland and analogues of it—Conan's own Cimmeria is the ur-heimat of the Gaels in Howard's mythos—were among Howard's favorite settings. Here he sets his tale among the historical Irish, in the reign of Brian Boru, first true High King of the Irish and the man who united them to humble the Scandinavian invaders who had pillaged them for centuries. A notable feature of the story is Howard's interpretation of Norse religion, here seen as a form of devil-worship owing more to his friend Lovecraft's evil beings from outer space than the actual faith of Asgard. Since their Irish victims regarded the Viking faith as demonic, there is a certain curious authenticity to this viewpoint. . . .

THE TWILIGHT OF THE GREY GODS

A voice echoed among the bleak reaches of the mountains that reared up gauntly on either hand. At the mouth of the defile that opened on a colossal crag, Conn the thrall wheeled, snarling like a wolf at bay. He was tall and massively, yet angrily, built, the fierceness of the wild dominant in his broad, sloping shoulders, his huge hairy chest and long, heavily muscled arms. His features were in keeping with his bodily aspect—a strong, stubborn jaw, low slanting forehead topped by a shock of tousled tawny hair which added to the wildness of his appearance no more than did his cold blue eyes. His only garment was a scanty loin-cloth. His own wolfish ruggedness was protection enough against the elements—for he was a slave in an age when even the masters lived lives as hard as the iron environments which bred them.

Now Conn half crouched, sword ready, a bestial snarl of menace humming in his bull-throat, and from the defile there came a tall man, wrapped in a cloak beneath which the thrall glimpsed a sheen of mail. The stranger wore a slouch hat pulled so low that from his shadowed features only one eye gleamed, cold and grim as the grey sea.

"Well, Conn, thrall of Wolfgar Snorri's son," said the stranger in a deep, powerful voice, "whither do you flee, with your master's blood on your hands?"

"I know you not," growled Conn, "nor how you know me. If you would take me, whistle up your dogs and make an end. Some of them will taste steel ere I die."

"Fool!" There was deep scorn in the reverberant tone. "I am no hunter of runaway serfs. There are wilder matters abroad. What do you smell in the seawind?"

Conn turned toward the sea, lapping greyly at

the cliffs far below. He expanded his mighty chest, his nostrils flaring as he breathed deeply.

"I smell the tang of salt-spume," he answered.

The stranger's voice was like the rasp of swords. "The scent of blood is on the wind—the musk of slaughter and the shouts of the slaying."

Conn shook his head, bewildered. "It is only the wind among the crags."

"There is war in your homeland," said the stranger somberly. "The spears of the South have risen against the swords of the North and the death-fires are lighting the land like the mid-day sun."

"How can you know this?" asked the thrall uneasily. "No ship has put in to Torka for weeks. Who are you? Whence come you? How know you these things?"

"Can you not hear the skirl of the pipes, the clashing of the axes?" replied the tall stranger. "Can you not smell the war-reek the wind brings?"

"Not I," answered Conn. "It is many a long league from Torka to Erin, and I hear only the wind among the crags and the gulls screeching over the headlands. Yet if there is war, I should be among the weapon-men of my clan, though my life is forfeit to Melaghlin because I slew a man of his in a quarrel."

The stranger gave no heed, standing like a statue as he gazed far out across the reaches of hazy barren mountains and misty waves.

"It is the death-grip," he said, like one who speaks to himself. "Now comes the reaping of kings, the garnering of chiefs like a harvest. Gigantic shadows stalk red-handed across the world, and night is falling on Asgaard. I hear the cries of long-dead heroes whistling in the void, and the shouts of forgotten gods. To each being there is an appointed time, and even the gods must die . . ."

He stiffened suddenly with a great shout, flinging his arms seaward. Tall, rolling clouds, sailing gigantically before the gale, veiled the sea. Out of the mist came a great wind and out of the wind a whirling mass of clouds. And Conn cried out. From out the flying clouds, shadowy and horrific, swept twelve shapes. He saw, as in a nightmare, the twelve winged horses and their riders, women in flaming silver mail and winged helmets, whose golden hair floated out on the wind behind them, and whose cold eyes were fixed on some awesome goal beyond his ken.

"The Choosers of the Slain!" thundered the stranger, flinging his arms wide in a terrible gesture. "They ride in the twilight of the North! The winged hooves spurn the rolling clouds, the web of Fate is spun, the Loom and Spindle broken! Doom roars upon the gods and night falls on Asgaard! Night and the trumpets of Ragnarok!"

The cloak was blown wide in the wind, revealing the mighty, mail-clad figure; the slouch hat fell aside; the wild elf-locks blew free. And Conn shrank before the blaze of the stranger's eye. And he saw that where the other eye should have been, was but an empty socket. Thereat panic seized him, so that he turned and ran down the defile as a man flees demons. And a fearsome backward glance showed him the stranger etched against the cloud-torn sky, cloak blowing in the wind, arms flung high, and it seemed to the thrall that the man had grown monstrously in stature, that he loomed colossal among the clouds, dwarfing the mountains and the sea, and that he was suddenly grey, as with vast age.

II

Oh Masters of the North, we come with tally
of remembered dead,
Of broken hearth and blazing home, and
rafters crashing overhead.
A single cast of dice we throw to balance, by
the leaden sea,
A hundred years of wrong and woe with one
red hour of butchery.

The spring gale had blown itself out. The sky smiled blue overhead and the sea lay placid as a pool, with only a few scattered bits of driftwood along the beaches to give mute evidence of her treachery. Along the strand rode a lone horseman, his saffron cloak whipping about behind him, his yellow hair blowing about his face in the breeze.

Suddenly he reined up so short that his spirited steed reared and snorted. From among the sand dunes had risen a man, tall and powerful, of wild, shock-headed aspect, and naked but for a loincloth.

"Who are you," demanded the horseman, "who bear the sword of a chief, yet have the appearance of a masterless man, and wear the collar of a serf withal?"

"I am Conn, young master," answered the

wanderer, "once an outlaw, once a thrall,—always a man of King Brian's, whether he will or no. And I know you. You are Dunlang O'Hartigan, friend of Murrogh, son of Brian, prince of Dal Cais. Tell me, good sir, is there war in the land?"

"Sooth to say," answered the young chief, "even now King Brian and King Malchi lie encamped at Kilmainham, before Dublin. I have but ridden from the camp this morning. From all the lands of the Vikings King Sitric of Dublin has summoned the slayers, and Gaels and Danes are ready to join battle—and such a battle as Erin has never seen before."

Conn's eyes clouded. "By Crom!" he muttered, half to himself, "It is even as the Grey Man said—yet how could he have known? Surely it was all a dream."

"How come you here?" asked Dunlang.

"From Torka in the Orkneys in an open boat, flung down as a chip is thrown upon the tide. Of yore I slew a man of Meath, kern of Melaghlin, and King Brian's heart was hot against me because of the broken truce; so I fled. Well, the life of an outlaw is hard. Thorwald Raven, Jarl of the Hebrides, took me when I was weak from hunger and wounds, and put this collar on my neck." The kern touched the heavy copper ring encircling his bull-neck. "Then he sold me to Wolfgar Snorri's son on Torka. He was a hard master. I did the work of three men, and stood at his back and mowed down carles like wheat when he brawled with his neighbors. In return he gave me crusts from his board, a bare earth floor to sleep on, and deep scars on my back. Finally I could bear it no more, and I leaped upon him in his own skalli and crushed his skull with a log of firewood. Then I took his sword and fled to the mountains, preferring to freeze or starve there rather than die under the lash.

"There in the mountains,"—again Conn's eyes clouded with doubt—"I think I dreamed," he said, "I saw a tall grey man who spoke of war in Erin, and in my dream I saw Valkyries riding southward on the clouds . . .

"Better to die at sea on a good venture than to starve in the Orkney mountains," he continued with more assurance, his feet on firm ground. "By chance I found a fisherman's boat, with a store of food and water, and I put to sea. By Crom! I wonder to find myself still alive! The gale took me in her fangs last night, and I know only that I fought the sea in the boat until the boat sank under my feet, and then fought her in her naked waves until my senses went from me. None could have been more surprised than I when I came to myself this dawn lying like a piece of driftwood on the beach. I have lain in the sun since, trying to warm the cold tang of the sea out of my bones."

"By the saints, Conn," said Dunlang, "I like your spirit."

"I hope King Brian likes it as well," grunted the kern.

"Attach yourself to my train," answered Dunlang. "I'll speak for you. King Brian has weightier matters on his mind than a single blood-feud. This very day the opposing hosts lie drawn up for the death-grip."

"Will the spear-shattering fall on the morrow?" asked Conn.

"Not by King Brian's will," answered Dunlang. "He is loath to shed blood on Good Friday. But who knows when the heathen will come down upon us?"

Conn laid a hand on Dunlang's stirrup-leather and strode beside him as the steed moved leisurely along.

"There is a notable gathering of weapon-men?"

"More than twenty thousand warriors on each side; the bay of Dublin is dark with the dragonships. From the Orkneys comes Jarl Sigurd with his raven banner. From Man comes the Viking Brodir with twenty longships. From the Danelagh in England comes Prince Amlaff, son of the King of Norway, with two thousand men. From all lands the hosts have gathered—from the Orkneys, the Shetlands, the Hebrides—from Scotland, England, Germany, and the lands of Scandinavia.

"Our spies say Sigurd and Brodir have a thousand men armed in steel mail from crown to heel, who fight in a solid wedge. The Dalcassians may be hard put to break that iron wall. Yet, God willing, we shall prevail. Then among the other chiefs and warriors there are Anrad the Berserk, Hrafn the Red, Platt of Danemark, Thorstein and his comrade-in-arms Asmund, Thorleif Hordi, the Strong, Athelstane the Saxon, and Thorwald Raven, Jarl of the Hebrides."

At that name Conn grinned savagely and fingered his copper collar. "It is a great gathering if both Sigurd and Brodir come."

"That was the doing of Gormlaith," responded Dunlang.

"Word had come to the Orkneys that Brian had divorced Kormlada," said Conn, unconsciously giving the queen her Norse name.

"Aye—and her heart is black with hate against him. Strange it is that a woman so fair of form and countenance should have the soul of a demon."

"God's truth, my lord. And what of her brother, Prince Mailmora?"

"Who but he is the instigator of the whole war?" cried Dunlang angrily. "The hate between him and Murrogh, so long smoldering, has at last burst into flame, firing both kingdoms. Both were in the wrong—Murrogh perhaps more than Mailmora. Gormlaith goaded her brother on. I did not believe King Brian acted wisely when he gave honors to those against whom he had warred. It was not well he married Gormlaith and gave his daughter to Gormlaith's son, Sitric of Dublin. With Gormlaith he took the seeds of strife and hatred into his palace. She is a wanton; once she was the wife of Amlaff Cauran, the Dane; then she was wife to King Malachi of Meath, and he put her aside because of her wickedness."

"What of Melaghlin?" asked Conn.

"He seems to have forgotten the struggle in which Brian wrested Erin's crown from him. Together the two kings move against the Danes and Mailmora."

As they conversed, they passed along the bare shore until they came into a rough broken stretch of cliffs and boulders; and there they halted suddenly. On a boulder sat a girl, clad in a shimmering green garment whose pattern was so much like scales that for a bewildered instant Conn thought himself gazing on a mermaid come out of the deeps.

"Eevin!" Dunlang swung down from his horse, tossing the reins to Conn, and advanced to take her slender hands in his. "You sent for me and I have come—you've been weeping!"

Conn, holding the steed, felt an impulse to retire, prompted by superstitious qualms. Eevin, with her slender form, her wealth of shimmering golden hair, and her deep mysterious eyes, was not like any other girl he had ever seen. Her entire aspect was different from the women of the Norse-folk and of the Gaels alike, and Conn knew her to be a member of that fading mystic race which had occupied the land before the coming of his ancestors, some of whom still dwelt in caverns along the sea and deep in unfrequented forests—the De Danaans, sorcerers, the Irish said, and kin to the faeries.

"Dunlang!" The girl caught her lover in a convulsive embrace. "You must not go into battle—the weird of far-sight is on me, and I know if you go to the war, you will die! Come away with me—I'll hide you—I'll show you dim purple caverns like the castles of deep-sea kings, and shadowy forests where none save my people has set foot. Come with me and forget wars and hates and prides and ambitions, which are but shadows without reality or substance. Come and learn the dreamy splendors of far places, where fear and hate are naught, and the years seem as hours, drifting forever."

"Eevin, my love!" cried Dunlang, troubled, "You ask that which is beyond my power. When my clan moves into battle, I must be at Murrogh's side, though sure death be my portion. I love you beyond all life, but by the honor of my clan, this is an impossible thing."

"I feared as much," she answered, resigned. "You of the Tall Folk are but children—foolish, cruel, violent—slaying one another in childish quarrels. This is punishment visited on me who, alone of all my people, have loved a man of the Tall Folk. Your rough hands have bruised my soft flesh unwittingly, and your rough spirit as unwittingly bruises my heart."

"I would not hurt you, Eevin," began Dunlang, pained.

"I know," she replied, "the hands of men are not made to handle the delicate body and heart of a woman of the Dark People. It is my fate. I love and I have lost. My sight is a far-sight which sees through the veil and the mists of life, behind the past and beyond the future. You will go into battle and the harps will keen for you; and Eevin of Craglea will weep until she melts in tears and the salt tears mingle with the cold salt sea."

Dunlang bowed his head, unspeaking, for her young voice vibrated with the ancient sorrow of womankind; and even the rough kern shuffled his feet uneasily.

"I have brought a gift against the time of battle," she went on, bending lithely to lift something which caught the sun's sheen. "It may not save you, the ghosts in my soul whisper—but I hope without hope in my heart."

Dunlang stared uncertainly at what she spread before him. Conn, edging closer and craning his neck, saw a hauberk of strange workmanship and a helmet such as he had never seen before,—a heavy affair made to slip over the entire head and rest on the neckpieces of the hauberk. There was no movable vizor, merely a slit cut in the front through which to see, and the workmanship was of an earlier, more civilized age, which no man living could duplicate.

Dunlang looked at it askance, with the characteristic Celtic antipathy toward armor. The Britons who faced Caesar's legionnaires fought naked, judging a man cowardly who cased himself in metal, and in later ages the Irish clans entertained the same conviction regarding Strongbow's mail-clad knights.

"Eevin," said Dunlang, "my brothers will laugh at me if I enclose myself in iron, like a Dane. How can a man have full freedom of limb, weighted by such a garment? Of all the Gaels, only Turlogh Dubh wears full mail."

"And is any man of the Gael less brave than he?" she cried passionately. "Oh, you of the Tall Folk are foolish! For ages the iron-clad Danes have trampled you, when you might have swept them out of the land long ago, but for your foolish pride."

"Not altogether pride, Eevin," argued Dunlang. "Of what avail is mail of plated armor against the Dalcassian ax which cuts through iron like cloth?"

"Mail would turn the swords of the Danes," she answered, "and not even an ax of the O'Briens would rend this armor. Long it has lain in the deep-sea caverns of my people, carefully protected from rust. He who wore it was a warrior of Rome in the long ago, before the legions were withdrawn from Britain. In an ancient war on the border of Wales, it fell into the hands of my people, and because its wearer was a great prince, my people treasured it. Now I beg you to wear it, if you love me."

Dunlang took it hesitantly, nor could he know that it was the armor worn by a gladiator in the days of the later Roman empire, nor wonder by what chance it had been worn by an officer in the British legion. Little of that knew Dunlang who, like most of his brother chiefs, could neither read nor write; knowledge and education were for monks and priests; a fighting man was kept too busy to cultivate the arts and sciences. He took the armor, and because he loved the strange girl, agreed to wear it—"if it will fit me."

"It will fit," she answered. "But I will see you no more alive."

She held out her white arms and he gathered her hungrily to him, while Conn looked away. Then Dunlang gently unlocked her clinging arms from about his neck, kissed her, and tore himself free.

Without a backward glance he mounted his steed and rode away, with Conn trotting easily alongside. Looking back in the gathering dusk, the kern saw Eevin standing there still, a poignant picture of despair.

III

The campfires sent up showers of sparks and illumined the land like day. In the distance loomed the grim walls of Dublin, dark and ominously silent; before the walls flickered other fires where the warriors of Leinster, under King Mailmora, whetted their axes for the coming battle. Out in the bay, the starlight glinted on myriad sails, shield-rails and arching serpent-prows. Between the city and the fires of the Irish host stretched the plain of Clontarf, bordered by Tomar's Wood, dark and rustling in the night, and the Liffey's dark, star-flecked waters.

Before his tent, the firelight playing on his white beard and glinting from his undimmed eagle eyes, sat the great King Brian Boru, among his chiefs. The king was old—seventy-three winters had passed over his lion-like head—long years crammed with fierce wars and bloody intrigues. Yet his back was straight, his arm unwithered, his voice deep and resonant. His chiefs stood about him, tall warriors with war-hardened hands and eyes whetted by the sun and the winds and the high places; tigerish princes in their rich tunics, green girdles, leathern sandals and saffron mantles caught with great golden brooches.

They were an array of war-eagles—Murrogh, Brian's eldest son, the pride of all Erin, tall and mighty, with wide blue eyes that were never placid, but danced with mirth, dulled with sadness, or blazed with fury; Murrogh's young son, Turlogh, a supple lad of fifteen with golden locks and an eager face—tense with anticipation of trying his hand for the first time in the great game of war.

And there was that other Turlogh, his cousin—Turlogh Dubh, who was only a few years older but who already had full stature and was famed throughout all Erin for his berserk rages and the cunning of his deadly ax-play. And there were Meathla O'Faelan, prince of Desmond or South Munster, and his kin—the Great Stewards of Scotland—Lennox, and Donald of Mar, who had crossed the Irish Channel with their wild Highlanders—tall men, sombre and gaunt and silent. And there were Dunlang O'Hartigan and O'Hyne, and prince of Hy Many, was in the tent of his uncle, King Malachi O'Neill, which was pitched in the camp of the Meathmen, apart from the Dalcassians, and King Brian was brooding on the matter. For since the setting of the sun, O'Kelly had been closeted with the King of Meath, and no man knew what passed between them.

Nor was Donagh, son of Brian, among the chiefs before the royal pavilion, for he was afield with a band ravaging the holdings of Mailmora of Leinster.

Now Dunlang approached the king, leading with him Conn, the kern.

"My Lord," quoth Dunlang, "here is a man who was outlawed aforetime, who has spent vile durance among the Gall, and who risked his life by storm and sea to return and fight under your banner. From the Orkneys in an open boat he came, naked and alone, and the sea cast him all but lifeless on the sand."

Brian stiffened; even in small things his memory was sharp as a whetted stone. "Thou!" he cried. "Aye, I remember him. Well, Conn, you have come back—and with your red hands!"

"Aye, King Brian," answered Conn stolidly, "my hands are red, it is true, and so I took to washing off the stain in Danish blood."

"You dare stand before me, to whom your life is forfeit!"

"This alone I know, King Brian," said Conn boldly, "my father was with you at Sulcoit and the sack of Limerick, and before that followed you in your days of wandering and was one of the fifteen warriors who remained to you when King Mahon, your brother, came seeking you in the forest. And my grandsire followed Murkertagh of the Leather Cloaks, and my people have fought the Danes since the days of Thorgils. You need men who can strike strong blows, and it is my right to die in battle against my ancient enemies, rather than shamefully at the end of a rope."

King Brian nodded. "Well spoken. Take your life. Your days of outlawry are at an end. King Malachi would perhaps think otherwise, since it was a man of his you slew, but—" He paused; an old doubt ate at his soul at the thought of the King of Meath. "Let it be," he went on, "let it rest until after the battle— mayhap that will be world's end for us all."

Dunlang stepped toward Conn and laid hand on the copper collar. "Let us cut this away; you are a free man now."

But Conn shook his head. "Not until I have slain Thorwald Raven who put it there. I'll wear it into battle as a sign of no quarter."

"That is a noble sword you wear, kern," said Murrogh suddenly.

"Aye, my Lord. Murkertagh of the Leather Cloaks wielded this blade until Blacair the Dane slew him at Ardee, and it remained in the possession of the Gall until I took it from the body of Wolfgar Snorri's son."

"It is not fitting that a kern should wear the sword of a king," said Murrogh brusquely. "Let one of the chiefs take it and give him an ax instead."

Conn's fingers locked about the hilt. "He would take the sword from me had best give me the ax first," he said grimly, "and that suddenly."

Murrogh's hot temper blazed. With an oath, he strode toward Conn, who met him eye to eye and gave back not a step.

"Be at ease, my son," ordered King Brian. "Let the kern keep the blade."

Murrogh struggled. His mood changed. "Aye, keep it and follow me into battle. We shall see if a king's sword in a kern's hand can hew as wide a path as a prince's blade."

"My lords," said Conn, "it may be God's will that I fall in the first onset—but the scars of slavery burn deep in my back this night, and I will not be backward when the spears are splintering."

IV

"Therefore your doom is on you,
Is on you and your kings...."

CHESTERTON

While King Brian communed with his chiefs on the plains above Clontarf, a grisly ritual was being enacted within the gloomy castle that was at once the fortress and palace of Dublin's king. With good reason did Christians fear and hate those grim walls; Dublin was a pagan city, ruled by savage heathen kings, and dark were the deeds committed therein.

In an inner chamber in the castle stood the Viking Brodir, sombrely watching a ghastly sacrifice on a grim black altar. On that monstrous stone writhed a naked, frothing thing that had been a comely youth; brutally bound and gagged, he could only twist convulsively beneath the dripping, inexorable dagger in the hands of the white-bearded wild-eyed priest of Odin.

The blade hacked through flesh and thew and bone; blood gushed, to be caught in a broad, copper bowl, which the priest, with his red-dappled beard, held high, invoking Odin in a frenzied chant. His thin, bony fingers tore the yet pulsing heart from the butchered breast, and his wild half-man eyes scanned it with avid intensity.

"What of your divinations?" demanded Brodir impatiently.

Shadows flickered in the priest's cold eyes, and his flesh crawled with a mysterious horror. "Fifty years I have served Odin," he said, "fifty years divined by the bleeding heart, but never such portents as these. Hark, Brodir! If ye fight not on Good Friday, as the Christians call it, your host will be utterly routed and all your chiefs slain; if ye fight on Good Friday, King Brian will die—but he will win the day."

Brodir cursed with cold venom.

The priest shook his ancient head. "I cannot fathom the portent—and I am the last of the priests of the Flaming Circle, who learned mysteries at the feet of Thorgils. I see battle and slaughter—and yet more—shapes gigantic and terrible that stalk monstrously through the mists ..."

"Enough of such mummery," snarled Brodir. "If I fall I would take Brian to Helheim with me. We go against the Gaels on the morrow, fall fair, fall foul!" He turned and strode from the room.

Brodir traversed a winding corridor and entered another, more spacious chamber, adorned, like all the Dublin king's palace, with the loot of all the world—gold-chased weapons, rare tapestries, rich rugs, divans from Byzantium and the East plunder taken from all peoples by the roving Norsemen; for Dublin was the center of the Vikings' wide-flung world, the headquarters whence they fared forth to loot the kings of the earth.

A queenly form rose to greet him. Kormlada, whom the Gaels called Gormlaith, was indeed fair, but there was cruelty in her face and in her hard, scintillant eyes. She was of mixed Irish and Danish blood, and looked the part of a barbaric queen, with her pendant earrings, her golden armlets and anklets, and her silver breastplates set with jewels. But for these breastplates, her only garments were a short silken skirt which came half way to her knees and was held in place by a wide girdle about her lithe waist, and sandals of soft red leather. Her hair was red-gold, her eyes light grey and glittering. Queen she had been, of Dublin, of Meath, and of Thomond. And queen she was still, for she held her son Sitric and her brother Mailmora in the palm of her slim white hand. Carried off in a raid in her childhood by Amlaff Cauran, King of Dublin, she had early discovered her power over men. As the child-wife of the rough Dane, she had swayed his kingdom at will, and her ambitions increased with her power.

Now she faced Brodir with her alluring, mysterious smile, but secret uneasiness ate at her. In all the world there was but one woman she feared, and but one man. And the man was Brodir. With him she was never entirely certain of her course; she duped him as she duped all men, but it was with many misgivings, for she sensed in him an elemental savagery which, once loosed, she might not be able to control.

"What of the priest's words, Brodir?" she asked.

"If we avoid battle on the morrow we lose," the Viking answered moodily. "If we fight, Brian wins, but falls. We fight, the more because my spies tell me Donagh is away from camp with a strong band, ravaging Mailmora's lands. We have sent spies to Malachi, who has an old grudge against Brian, urging him to desert the king—or at least to stand aside and aid neither of us. We have offered him rich rewards and Brian's lands to rule. Ha! Let him step into our trap! Not gold, but a bloody sword we will give him. With Brian crushed we will turn on Malachi and tread him into the dust! But first—Brian."

She clenched her white hands in savage exultation. "Bring me his head! I'll hang it above our bridal bed."

"I have heard strange tales," said Brodir soberly. "Sigurd has boasted in his cups."

Kormlada started and scanned the inscrutable countenance. Again she felt a quiver of fear as she gazed at the sombre Viking with his tall, strong stature, his dark, menacing face, and his heavy black locks which he wore braided and caught in his sword-belt.

"What has Sigurd said?" she asked, striving to make her voice casual.

"When Sitric came to me in my skalli on the Isle of Man," said Brodir, red glints beginning to smoulder in his dark eyes, "it was his oath that if I came to his aid, I should sit on the throne of Ireland with you as my queen. Now that fool of an Orkneyman, Sigurd, boasts in his ale that he was promised the same reward."

She forced a laugh. "He was drunk."

Brodir burst into wild cursing as the violence of the untamed Viking surged up in him. "You lie, you wanton!" he shouted, seizing her white wrist in an iron grip. "You were born to lure men to their doom! But you will not play fast and loose with Brodir of Man!"

"You are mad!" she cried, twisting vainly in his grasp. "Release me, or I'll call my guards!"

"Call them!" he snarled, "and I'll slash the heads from their bodies. Cross me now and blood will run ankle-deep in Dublin's streets. By Thor! there will be no city left for Brian to burn! Mailmora, Sitric, Sigurd, Amlaff—I'll cut all their throats and drag you naked to my ship by your yellow hair. Dare to call out!"

She dared not. He forced her to her knees, twisting her white arm so brutally that she bit her lip to keep from screaming.

"You promised Sigurd the same thing you promised me," he went on in ill-controlled fury, "knowing neither of us would throw away his life for less!"

"No! No!" she shrieked. "I swear by the ring of Thor!" Then, as the agony grew unbearable, she dropped pretense. "Yes—yes, I promised him—oh, let me go!"

"So!" The Viking tossed her contemptuously on to a pile of silken cushions, where she lay whimpering and disheveled. "You promised me and you promised Sigurd," he said, looming menacingly above her, "but your promise to me you'll keep—else you had better never been born. The throne of Ireland is a small thing beside my desire for you—if I cannot have you, no one shall."

"But what of Sigurd?"

"He'll fall in battle—or afterward," he answered grimly.

"Good enough!" Dire indeed was the extremity in which Kormlada had not her wits about her. "It's you I love, Brodir; I promised him only because he would not aid us otherwise."

"Love!" The Viking laughed savagely. "You love Kormlada—none other. But you'll keep your vow to me or you'll rue it." And, turning on his heel, he left her chamber.

Kormlada rose, rubbing her arm where the blue marks of his fingers marred her skin. "May he fall in the first charge!" she ground between her teeth. "If either survive, may it be that tall fool, Sigurd—methinks he would be a husband easier to manage than that black-haired savage. I will perforce marry him if he survives the battle, but by Thor! he shall not long press the throne of Ireland—I'll send him to join Brian."

"You speak as though King Brian were already dead." A tranquil voice behind Kormlada brought her about to face the other person in the world she feared besides Brodir. Her eyes widened as they fell upon a slender girl clad in shimmering green, a girl whose golden hair glimmered with unearthly light in the glow of the candles. The queen recoiled, hands outstretched as if to fend her away.

"Eevin! Stand back, witch! Cast no spell on me! How came you into my palace?"

"How came the breeze through the trees?" answered the Danaan girl. "What was Brodir saying to you before I entered?"

"If you are a sorceress, you know," suddenly answered the queen.

Eevin nodded. "Aye, I know. In your own mind I read it. He had consulted the oracle of the sea-people—the blood and the torn heart,"—her dainty lips curled with disgust—"and he told you he would attack tomorrow."

The queen blenched and made no reply, fearing to meet Eevin's magnetic eyes. She felt naked before the mysterious girl who could uncannily sift the contents of her mind and empty it of its secrets.

Eevin stood with bent head for a moment, then raised her head suddenly. Kormlada started, for something akin to fear shone in the were-girl's eyes.

"Who is in this castle?" she cried.

"You know as well as I," muttered Kormlada. "Sitric, Sigurd, Brodir."

"There is another!" exclaimed Eevin, paling and

shuddering. "Ah, I know him of old—I feel him—he bears the cold of the North with him, the shivering tang of icy seas . . ."

She turned and slipped swiftly through the velvet hangings that masked a hidden doorway Kormlada had thought known only to herself and her women, leaving the queen bewildered and uneasy.

In the sacrificial chamber, the ancient priest still mumbled over the gory altar upon which lay the mutilated victim of his rite. "Fifty years I have served Odin," he maundered. "And never such portents have I read. Odin laid his mark upon me long ago in a night of horror. The years fall like withered leaves, and my age draws to a close. One by one I have seen the altars of Odin crumble. If the Christians win this battle, Odin's day is done. It comes upon me that I have offered up my last sacrifice . . ."

A deep, powerful voice spoke behind him. "And what more fitting than that you should accompany the soul of that last sacrifice to the realm of him you served?"

The priest wheeled, the sacrificial dagger falling from his hand. Before him stood a tall man, wrapped in a cloak beneath which shone the gleam of armor. A slouch hat was pulled low over his forehead, and when he pushed it back, a single eye, glittering and grim as the grey sea, met his horrified gaze.

Warriors who rushed into the chamber at the strangled scream that burst hideously forth, found the old priest dead beside his corpse-laden altar, unwounded, but with face and body shrivelled as by some intolerable exposure, and a soul-shaking horror in his glassy eyes. Yet, save for the corpses, the chamber was empty, and none had been seen to enter it since Brodir had gone forth.

Alone in his tent with the heavily-armed galla-glachs ranged outside, King Brian was dreaming a strange dream. In his dream a tall grey giant loomed terribly above him, and cried in a voice that was like thunder among the clouds, "Beware, champion of the white Christ! Though you smite my children with the sword and drive me into the dark voids of Jotunheim, yet shall I work you rue! As you smite my children with the sword, so shall I smite the son of your body, and as I go into the dark, so shall you go likewise, when the Choosers of the Slain ride the clouds above the battlefield!"

The thunder of the giant's voice and the awesome glitter of his single eye froze the blood of the king who had never known fear, and with a strangled cry, he woke, starting up. The thick torches which burned outside illumined the interior of his tent sufficiently well for him to make out a slender form.

"Eevin!" he cried. "By my soul! it is well for kings that your people take no part in the intrigues of mortals, when you can steal under the very noses of the guards into our tents. Do you seek Dunlang?"

The girl shook her head sadly. "I see him no more alive, great king. Were I to go to him now, my own black sorrow might unman him. I will come to him among the dead tomorrow."

King Brian shivered.

"But it is not of my woes that I came to speak, My Lord," she continued wearily. "It is not the way of the Dark People to take part in the quarrels of the Tall Folk—but I love one of them. This night I talked with Gormlaith."

Brian winced at the name of his divorced queen. "And your news?" he asked.

"Brodir strikes on the morrow."

The king shook his head heavily. "It vexes my soul to spill blood on the Holy Day. But if God wills it, we will not await their onslaught—we will march at dawn to meet them. I will send a swift runner to bring back Donagh . . ."

Eevin shook her head once more. "Nay, great king. Let Donagh live. After the battle the Dalcassians will need strong arms to brace the sceptre."

Brian gazed fixedly at her. "I read my doom in those words. Have you cast my fate?"

Eevin spread her hands helplessly. "My Lord, not even the Dark People can rend the Veil at will. Not by the casting of fates, or the sorcery of divination, not in smoke or in blood have I read it, but a weird is upon me and I see through flame and the dim clash of battle."

"And I shall fall?"

She bowed her face in her hands.

"Well, let it fall as God wills," said King Brian tranquilly. "I have lived long and deeply. Weep not—through the darkest mists of gloom and night, dawn yet rises on the world. My clan will revere you in the long days to come. Now go, for the night wanes toward morn, and I would make my peace with God."

And Eevin of Craglea went like a shadow from the king's tent.

V

The war was like a dream; I cannot tell
How many heathens souls I sent to Hell.
I only know, above the fallen ones
I heard dark Odin shouting to his sons,
And felt amid the battle's roar and shock
The strive of gods that crashed in Ragnarok.

—CONN'S SAGA

Through the mist of the whitening dawn men moved like ghosts and weapons clanked eerily. Conn stretched his muscular arms, yawned cavernously, and loosened his great blade in its sheath. "This is the day the ravens drink blood, My Lord," he said, and Dunlang O'Hartigan nodded absently.

"Come hither and aid me to don this cursed cage," said the young chief. "For Eevin's sake I'll wear it; but by the saints! I had rather battle stark naked!"

The Gaels were on the move, marching from Kilmainham in the same formation in which they intended to enter battle. First came the Dalcassians, big rangy men in their saffron tunics, with a round buckler of steel-braced yew wood on the left arm, and the right hand gripping the dreaded Dalcassian ax. This ax differed greatly from the heavy weapon of the Danes; the Irish wielded it with one hand, the thumb stretched along the haft to guide the blow, and they had attained a skill at ax-fighting never before or since equalled. Hauberks they had none, neither the gallaglachs nor the kerns, though some of their chiefs, like Murrogh, wore light steel caps. But the tunics of warriors and chiefs alike had been woven with such skill and steeped in vinegar until their remarkable toughness afforded some protection against sword and arrow.

At the head of the Dalcassians strode Prince Murrogh, his fierce eyes alight, smiling as though he went to a feast instead of a slaughtering. On one side went Dunlang in his Roman corselet, closely followed by Conn, bearing the helmet, and on the other the two Turloghs—the son of Murrogh, and Turlogh Dubh, who alone of all the Dalcassians always went into battle fully armored. He looked grim enough, despite his youth, with his dark face and smoldering blue eyes, clad as he was in a full shirt of black mail, mail leggings and a steel helmet with a mail drop, and bearing a spiked buckler. Unlike the rest of the chiefs, who preferred their swords in battle, Black Turlogh fought with an ax of his own forging, and his skill with the weapon was almost uncanny.

Close behind the Dalcassians were the two companies of the Scottish, with their chiefs, the Great Stewards of Scotland, who, veterans of long wars with the Saxons, wore helmets with horsehair crests and coats of mail. With them came the men of South Munster commanded by Prince Meathla O'Faelan.

The third division consisted of the warriors of Connacht, wild men of the west, shock-headed and naked but for their wolf-skins, with their chiefs O'Kelly and O'Hyne. O'Kelly marched as a man whose soul is heavy, for the shadow of his meeting with Malachi the night before fell gauntly across him.

Somewhat apart from the three main divisions marched the tall gallaglachs and kerns of Meath, their king riding slowly before them.

And before all the host rode King Brian Boru on a white steed, his white locks blown about his ancient face and his eyes strange and fey, so that the wild kerns gazed on him with superstitious awe.

So the Gaels came before Dublin, where they saw the hosts of Leinster and Lochlann drawn up in battle array, stretching in a wide crescent from Dubhgall's Bridge to a narrow river Tolka which cuts the plain of Clontarf. Three main divisions there were—the foreign Northmen, the Vikings, with Sigurd and the grim Brodir; flanking them on the one side, the fierce Danes of Dublin, under their chief, a sombre wanderer whose name no man knew, but who was called Dubhgall, the Dark Stranger; and on the other flank the Irish of Leinster, with their king, Mailmora. The Danish fortress on the hill beyond the Liffey River bristled with armed men where King Sitric guarded the city.

There was but one way into the city from the north, the direction from which the Gaels were advancing, for in those days Dublin lay wholly south of the Liffey; that was the bridge called Dubhgall's Bridge. The Danes stood with one horn of their line guarding this entrance, their ranks curving out toward Tolka, their backs to the sea. The Gaels advanced along the level plain which stretched between Tomar's Wood and the shore.

With little more than a bow-shot separating the hosts, the Gaels halted, and King Brian rode in front of them, holding aloft a crucifix. "Sons of Goidhel!" his voice rang like a trumpet call. "It is not given me to lead you into the fray, as I led you in days of old. But I have pitched my tent behind your lines, where you must trample me if you flee. You will not flee! Remember a hundred years of outrage and infamy! Remember your burned homes, your slaughtered kin, your ravaged women, your babes enslaved! Before you stand your oppressors! On this day our good Lord died for you! There stand the heathen hordes which revile His Name and slay His people! I have but one command to give you—conquer or die!"

The wild hordes yelled like wolves and a forest of axes brandished on high. King Brian bowed his head and his face was grey.

"Let them lead me back to my tent," he whispered to Murrogh. "Age has withered me from the play of the axes and my doom is hard upon me. Go forth, and may God stiffen your arms to the slaying!"

Now as the king rode slowly back to his tent among his guardsmen, there was a taking up of girdles, a drawing of blades, a dressing of shields. Conn placed the Roman helmet on Dunlang's head and grinned at the result, for the young chief looked like some mythical iron monster out of

Norse legendry. The hosts moved inexorably toward each other.

The Vikings had assumed their favorite wedge-shaped formation with Sigurd and Brodir at the tip. The Northmen offered a strong contrast to the loose lines of the half-naked Gaels. They moved in compact ranks, armored with horned helmets, heavy scale-mail coats reaching to their knees, and leggings of seasoned wolf-hide braced with iron plates; and they bore great kite-shaped shields of linden wood with iron rims, and long spears. The thousand warriors in the forefront wore long leggings and gauntlets of mail as well, so that from crown to heel they were steel-clad. These marched in a solid shield-wall, bucklers overlapping, and over their iron ranks floated the grim raven banner which had always brought victory to Jarl Sigurd—even if it brought death to the bearer. Now it was borne by old Rane Asgrimm's son, who felt that the hour of his death was at hand.

At the tip of the wedge, like the point of a spear, were the champions of Lochlann—Brodir in his dully glittering blue mail, which no blade had even dented; Jarl Sigurd, tall, blond-bearded, gleaming in his golden-scaled hauberk; Hrafn the Red, in whose soul lurked a mocking devil that moved him to gargantuan laughter even in the madness of battle; the tall comrades, Thorstein and Asmund; Prince Amlaff, roving son of the King of Norway; Platt of Danemark; Athelstane the Saxon; Jarl Thorwald Raven of the Hebrides; Anrad the Berserk.

Toward this formidable array the Irish advanced at quick pace in more or less open formation and with scant attempt at any orderly ranks. But Malachi and his warriors wheeled suddenly and drew off to the extreme left, taking up their position on the high ground by Cabra. And when Murrogh saw this, he cursed under his breath, and Black Turlogh growled, "Who said an O'Neill forgets an old grudge? By Crom! Murrogh, we may have to guard our backs as well as our breasts before this fight be won!"

Now suddenly from the Viking ranks strode Platt of Danemark, his red hair like a crimson veil about his bare head, his silver mail gleaming. The hosts watched eagerly, for in those days few battles began without preliminary single combats.

"Donald!" shouted Platt, flinging up his naked sword so that the rising sun caught it in a sheen of silver. "Where is Donald of Mar? Are you there, Donald, as you were at Rhu Stoir, or do you skulk from the fray?"

"I am here, Rogue!" answered the Scottish chief as he strode, tall and gaunt, from among his men, flinging away his scabbard.

Highlander and Dane met in the middle space between the hosts, Donald cautious as a hunting wolf, Platt leaping in reckless and headlong, eyes alight and dancing with a laughing madness. Yet it was the wary Steward's foot which slipped suddenly on a rolling pebble, and before he could regain his balance, Platt's sword lunged into him so fiercely that the keen point tore through his corselet-scales and sank deep beneath his heart. Platt's mad yell of exultation broke in a gasp. Even as he crumpled, Donald of Mar lashed out a dying stroke that split the Dane's head, and the two fell together.

Thereat a deep-toned roar went up to the heavens, and the two great hosts rolled together like a tidal wave. Then were struck the first blows of the battle. There were no maneuvers of strategy, no cavalry charges, no flights of arrows. Forty thousand men fought on foot, hand to hand, man to man, slaying and dying in red chaos. The battle broke in howling waves about the spears and axes of the warriors. The first to shock were the Dalcassians and the Vikings, and as they met, both lines rocked at the impact. The deep roar of the Norsemen mingled with the yells of the Gaels and the Northern spears splintered among the Western axes. Foremost in the fray, Murrogh's great body heaved and strained as he roared and smote right and left with a heavy sword in either hand, mowing down men like corn. Neither shield nor helmet stood beneath his terrible blows, and behind him came his warriors slashing and howling like devils. Against the compact lines of the Dublin Danes thundered the wild tribesmen of Connacht, and the men of South Munster and their Scottish allies fell vengefully upon the Irish of Leinster.

The iron lines writhed and interwove across the plain. Conn, following Dunlang, grinned savagely as he smote home with dripping blade, and his fierce eyes sought for Thorwald Raven among the spears. But in that mad sea of battle where wild faces came and went like waves, it was difficult to pick out any one man.

At first both lines held without giving an inch; feet braced, straining breast to breast, they snarled and hacked, shield jammed hard against shield. All up and down the line of battle blades shimmered and flashed like sea-spray in the sun, and the roar of battle shook the ravens that wheeled like Valkyries overhead. Then, when human flesh and blood could stand no more, the serried lines began to roll forward or back. The Leinstermen flinched before the fierce onslaught of the Munster clans and their Scottish allies, giving way slowly, foot by foot, cursed by their king, who fought on foot with a sword in the forefront of the fray.

But on the other flanks, the Danes of Dublin under the redoubtable Dubhgall had held against the first blasting charge of the Western tribes, though their ranks reeled at the shock, and now the wild men in their wolf-skins were falling like garnered grain before the Danish axes.

In the center, the battle raged most fiercely; the wedged-shaped shield-wall of the Vikings held, and against its iron ranks the Dalcassians hurled their half-naked bodies in vain. A ghastly heap ringed that rim wall as Brodir and Sigurd began a slow, steady advance, the inexorable outstride of the Vikings, hacking deeper and deeper into the loose formation of the Gaels.

On the walls of Dublin Castle, King Sitric, watching the fight with Kormlada and his wife, exclaimed, "Well do the sea-kings reap the field!"

Kormlada's beautiful eyes blazed with wild exultation. "Fall, Brian!" she cried fiercely. "Fall, Murrogh! And fall too, Brodir! Let the keen ravens feed!" Her voice faltered as her eyes fell upon a tall cloaked figure standing on the battlements, apart from the people—a sombre grey giant, brooding over the battle. A cold fear stole over her and froze the words on her lips. She plucked at Sitric's cloak. "Who is he?" she whispered, pointing.

Sitric looked and shuddered. "I know not. Pay him no heed. Go not near him. When I but approached him, he spoke not or looked at me, but a cold wind blew over me and my heart shrivelled. Let us rather watch the battle. The Gaels give way."

But at the foremost point of the Gaelic advance, the line held. There, like the convex center of a curving ax-blade, fought Murrogh and his chiefs. The great prince was already streaming blood from gashes on his limbs, but his heavy swords flamed in double strokes that dealt death like a harvest, and the chiefs at his side mowed down the corn of battle. Fiercely Murrogh sought to reach Sigurd through the press. He saw the tall Jarl looming across the waves of spears and heads, striking blows like thunder-strokes, and the sight drove the Gaelic prince to madness. But he could not reach the Viking.

"The warriors are forced back," gasped Dunlang, seeking to shake the sweat from his eyes. The young chief was untouched; spears and axes alike splintered on the Roman helmet or glanced from the ancient cuirass, but, unused to armor, he felt like a chained wolf.

Murrogh spared a single swift glance; on either side of the clump of chiefs, the gallaglachs were falling back, slowly, savagely, selling each foot of ground with blood, unable to halt the irresistible advance of the mailed Northmen. These were falling, too, all along the battle-line, but they closed ranks and forced their way forward, legs braced hard, bodies strained, spears driving without cease or pause; they plowed on through a red surf of dead and dying.

"Turlogh!" gasped Murrogh, dashing the blood from his eyes. "Haste from the fray for Malachi! Bid him charge, in God's name!"

But the frenzy of slaughter was on Black Turlogh; froth flecked his lips and his eyes were those of a madman. "The Devil take Malachi!" he shouted, splitting a Dane's skull with a stroke like the slash of a tiger's paw.

"Conn!" called Murrogh, and as he spoke he gripped the big kern's shoulder and dragged him back. "Haste to Malachi—we need his support."

Conn drew reluctantly away from the melee, clearing his path with thunderous strokes. Across the reeling sea of blades and rocking helmets he saw the towering form of Jarl Sigurd and his lords—the billowing folds of the raven banner floated above them as their whistling swords hewed down men like wheat before the reaper.

Free of the press, the kern ran swiftly along the battle-line until he came to the higher ground of Cabra where the Meathmen thronged, tense and trembling like hunting hounds as they gripped their weapons and looked eagerly at their king. Malachi stood apart, watching the fray with moody eyes, his lion's head bowed, his fingers twined in his golden beard.

"King Melaghlin," said Conn bluntly, "Prince Murrogh urges you to charge home, for the press is great and the men of the Gael are hard beset."

The great O'Neill lifted his head and stared absently at the kern. Conn little guessed the chaotic struggle which was taking place in Malachi's soul—the red visions which thronged his brain—riches, power, the rule of all Erin, balanced against the black shame of treachery. He gazed out across the field where the banner of his nephew O'Kelly heaved among the spears. And Malachi shuddered, but shook his head.

"Nay," he said, "it is not time. I will charge—when the time comes."

For an instant king and kern looked into each others' eyes. Malachi's eyes dropped. Conn turned without a word and sped down the slope. As he went, he saw that the advance of Lennox and the men of Desmond had been checked. Mailmora, raging like a wild man, had cut down Prince Meathla O'Faelan with his own hand, a chance spear-thrust had wounded the Great Steward, and now the Leinstermen held fast against the onset of the Munster and Scottish clans. But where the Dalcassians fought, the battle was locked; the Prince of Thomond broke the onrush of the Norsemen like a jutting cliff that breaks the sea.

Conn reached Murrogh in the upheaval of slaughter. "Melaghlin says he will charge when the time comes."

"Hell to his soul!" cried Black Turlogh. "We are betrayed!"

Murrogh's blue eyes flamed. "Then in the name of God!" he roared, "Let us charge and die!"

The struggling men were stirred at his shout. The blind passion of the Gael surged up, bred of desperation; the lines stiffened, and a great shout shook the field that made King Sitric on his castle wall whiten and grip the parapet. He had heard such shouting before.

Now, as Murrogh leaped forward, the Gaels awoke to red fury as in men who have no hope. The nearness of doom woke frenzy in them, and, like inspired madmen, they hurled their last charge and smote the wall of shields, which reeled at the blow. No human power could stay the onslaught. Murrogh and his chiefs no longer hoped to win, or even to live, but only to glut their fury as they died, and in their despair they fought like wounded tigers—severing limbs, splitting skulls, cleaving breasts and shoulder-bones. Close at Murrogh's heels, flamed the ax of Black Turlogh and the swords of Dunlang and the chiefs; under that torrent of steel the iron line crumpled and gave, and through the breach the frenzied Gaels poured. The shield formation melted away.

At the same moment the wild men of Connacht again hurled a desperate charge against the Dublin Danes. O'Hyne and Dubhgall fell together and the Dublin men were battered backward, disputing every foot. The whole field melted into a mingled mass of slashing battlers without rank or formation. Among a heap of torn Dalcassian dead, Murrogh came at last upon Jarl Sigurd. Behind the Jarl stood grim old Rane Asgrimm's son, holding the raven banner. Murrogh slew him with a single stroke. Sigurd turned, and his sword rent Murrogh's tunic and gashed his chest, but the Irish prince smote so fiercely on the Norseman's shield that Jarl Sigurd reeled backward.

Thorleif Hordi had picked up the banner, but

scarce had he lifted it when Black Turlogh, his eyes glaring, broke through and split his skull to the teeth. Sigurd, seeing his banner fallen once more, struck Murrogh with such desperate fury that his sword bit through the prince's morion and gashed his scalp. Blood jetted down Murrogh's face, and he reeled, but before Sigurd could strike again, Black Turlogh's ax licked out like a flicker of lightning. The Jarl's warding shield fell shattered from his arm, and Sigurd gave back for an instant, daunted by the play of that deathly ax. Then a rush of warriors swept the ranging chiefs apart.

"Thorstein!" shouted Sigurd. "Take up the banner!"

"Touch it not!" cried Asmund. "Who bears it, dies!" Even as he spoke, Dunlang's sword crushed his skull.

"Hrafn!" called Sigurd desperately. "Bear the banner!"

"Bear your own curse!" answered Hrafn. "This is the end of us all."

"Cowards!" roared the Jarl, snatching up the banner himself and striving to gather it under his cloak as Murrogh, face bloodied and eyes blazing, broke through to him. Sigurd flung up his sword—too late. The weapon in Murrogh's right hand splintered on his helmet, bursting the straps that held it and ripping it from his head, and Murrogh's left-hand sword, whistling in behind the first blow, shattered the Jarl's skull and felled him dead in the bloody folds of the great banner that wrapped about him as he went down.

Now a great roar went up, and the Gaels

redoubled their strokes. With the formation of shields torn apart, the mail of the Vikings could not save them; for the Dalcassian axes, flashing in the sun, hewed through chainmesh and iron plates alike, rending linden shield and horned helmet. Yet the Danes did not break.

On the high ramparts, King Sitric had turned pale, his hands trembling where he gripped the parapet. He knew that these wild men could not be beaten now, for they spilled their lives like water, hurling their naked bodies again and again into the fangs of spear and ax. Kormlada was silent, but Sitric's wife, King Brian's daughter, cried out in joy, for her heart was with her own people.

Murrogh was striving now to reach Brodir, but the black Viking had seen Sigurd die. Brodir's world was crumbling; even his vaunted mail was failing him, for though it had thus far saved his skin, it was tattered now. Never before had the Manx Viking faced the dreaded Dalcassian ax. He drew back from Murrogh's onset. In the crush, an ax shattered on Murrogh's helmet, knocking him to his knees and blinding him momentarily with its impact. Dunlang's sword wove a wheel of death above the fallen prince, and Murrogh reeled up.

The press slackened as Black Turlogh, Conn and young Turlogh drove in, hacking and stabbing, and Dunlang, frenzied by the heat of battle, tore off his helmet and flung it aside, ripping off his cuirass.

"The Devil eat such cages!" he shouted, catching at the reeling prince to support him, and even at that instant Thorstein the Dane ran in and drove his spear into Dunlang's side. The young Dalcassian staggered and fell at Murrogh's feet, and Conn leaped forward to strike Thorstein's head from his shoulders so that it whirled grinning still through the air in a shower of crimson.

Murrogh shook the darkness from his eyes. "Dunlang!" he cried in a fearful voice, falling to his knees at his friend's side and raising his head.

But Dunlang's eyes were already glazing. "Murrogh! Eevin!" Then blood gushed from his lips and he went limp in Murrogh's arms.

Murrogh leaped up with a shout of demoniac fury. He rushed into the thick of the Vikings, and his men swept in behind him.

On the hill of Cabra, Malachi cried out, flinging doubts and plots to the wind. As Brodir had plotted, so had he. He had but to stand aside until both hosts were cut to pieces, then seize Erin, tricking the Danes as they had planned to betray him. But his blood cried out against him and would not be stilled. He gripped the golden collar of Tomar about his neck, the collar he had taken so many years before from the Danish king his sword had broken, and the old fire leaped up.

"Charge and die!" he shouted, drawing his sword, and at his back the men of Meath gave tongue like a hunting back and swarmed down into the field.

Under the shock of the Meathmen's assault, the weakened Danes staggered and broke. They tore away singly and in desperate slashing groups, seeking to gain the bay where their ships were anchored. But the Meathmen had cut off their retreat, and the ships lay far out, for the tide was at flood. All day that terrific battle had ranged, yet to Conn, snatching a startled glance at the setting sun, it seemed that scarce an hour had passed since the first lines had crashed together.

The fleeing Northmen made for the river, and the Gaels plunged in after them to drag them down. Among the fugitives and the groups of Norsemen who here and there made determined stands, the Irish chiefs were divided. The boy Turlogh was separated from Murrogh's side and vanished in the Tolka, struggling with a Dane. The clans of Leinster did not break until Black Turlogh rushed like a maddened beast into the thick of them and struck Mailmora dead in the midst of his warriors.

Murrogh, still blood-mad, but staggering from fatigue and weakened by loss of blood, came upon a band of Vikings who, back to back, resisted the conquerors. Their leader was Anrad the Berserk, who, when he saw Murrogh, rushed furiously upon him. Murrogh, too weary to parry the Dane's stroke, dropped his own sword and closed with Anrad, bearing him to the ground. The sword was wrenched from the Dane's hand as they fell. Both snatched at it, but Murrogh caught the hilt and Anrad the blade. The Gaelic prince tore it away, dragging the keen edge through the Viking's hand, severing nerve and thew; and, setting a knee on Anrad's chest, Murrogh drove the sword thrice through his body. Anrad, dying, drew a dagger, but his strength ebbed so swiftly that his arm sank. And then a mighty hand gripped his wrist and drove home the stroke he had sought to strike, so that the keen blade sank beneath Murrogh's heart.

Murrogh fell back dying, and his last glance showed him a tall grey giant looming above, his cloak billowing in the wind, his one glittering eye cold and terrible. But the mazed eyes of the surrounding warriors saw only death and the dealing of death.

The Danes were all in flight now, and on the high wall King Sitric sat watching his high ambitions fade away, while Kormlada gazed wild-eyed into ruin, defeat and shame.

Conn ran among the dying and fleeing, seeking Thorwald Raven. The kern's buckler was gone, shattered among the axes. His broad breast was gashed in half a dozen places; a sword-edge had bitten into his scalp when only his shock of tangled hair had saved him. A spear had girded into his thigh. Yet now in this heat and fury he scarcely felt those wounds.

A weakening hand caught at Conn's knee as he stumbled among dead men in wolf-skins and mailed corpses. He bent and saw O'Kelly, Malachi's nephew, and chief of the Hy Many. The chief's eyes were glazing in death. Conn lifted his head, and a smile curled the blue lips.

"I hear the war-cry of the O'Neill," he whispered. "Malachi could not betray us. He could not stand from the fray. The Red Hand-to-Victory!"

Conn rose as O'Kelly died, and caught sight of a familiar figure. Thorwald Raven had broken from the press and now fled alone and swiftly, not toward the sea or the river, where his comrades died beneath the Gaelic axes, but toward Tomar's Wood. Conn followed, spurred by his hate.

Thorwald saw him, and turned, snarling. So the

thrall met his former master. As Conn rushed into close quarters, the Norseman gripped his spear-shaft with both hands and lunged fiercely, but the point glanced from the great copper collar about the kern's neck. Conn, bending low, lunged upward with all his power, so that the great blade ripped through Jarl Thorwald's tattered mail and spilled his entrails on the ground.

Turning, Conn saw that the chase had brought him almost to the king's tent, pitched behind the battle-lines. He saw King Brian Boru standing in front of the tent, his white locks flowing in the wind, and but one man attending him. Conn ran forward.

"Kern, what are your tidings?" asked the king.

"The foreigners flee," answered Conn. "But Murrogh has fallen."

"You bring evil tidings," said Brian. "Erin shall never again look on a champion like him." And age like a cold cloud closed upon him.

"Where are your guards, My Lord?" asked Conn.

"They have joined in the pursuit."

"Let me then take you to a safer place," said Conn. "The Gall fly all about us here."

King Brian shook his head. "Nay, I know I leave not this place alive, for Eevin of Craglea told me last night I should fall this day. And what avails me to survive Murrogh and the champions of the Gael? Let me lie at Armagh, in the peace of God."

Now the attendant cried out, "My king, we are undone! Men blue and naked are upon us."

"The armored Danes," cried Conn, wheeling.

King Brian drew his heavy sword.

A group of blood-stained Vikings were approaching, led by Brodir and Prince Amlaff. Their vaunted mail hung in shreds; their swords were notched and dripping. Brodir had marked the king's tent from afar, and was bent on murder, for his soul raged with shame and fury and he was beset by visions in which Brian, Sigurd, and Kormlada spun in a hellish dance. He had lost the battle, Ireland, Kormlada—now he was ready to give up his life in a dying stroke of vengeance.

Brodir rushed upon the king, Prince Amlaff at his heels. Conn sprang to bar their way. But Brodir swerved aside and left the kern to Amlaff, as he fell upon the king. Conn took Amlaff's blade in his left arm and smote a single terrible blow that rent the prince's hauberk like paper and shattered his spine. Then the kern sprang back to guard King Brian.

Then even as he turned, Conn saw Brodir parry Brian's stroke and drive his sword through the ancient king's breast. Dunn went down, but even as he fell he caught himself on one knee and thrust his keen blade through flesh and bone, cutting both Brodir's legs from under him. The Viking's scream of triumph broke in a ghastly groan as he toppled in a widening pool of crimson. There he struggled convulsively and lay still.

Conn stood looking dazedly around him. Brodir's company of men had fled, and the Gaels were converging on Brian's tent. The sound of the keening for the heroes already rose to mingle with the screams and shouts that still came from the struggling hordes along the river. They were bringing Murrogh's body to the king's tent, walking slowly—weary, bloody, men with bowed heads. Behind the litter that bore the prince's body came others—laden with the bodies of Turlogh, Murrogh's son; of Donald, Steward of Mar; of O'Kelly and O'Hyne, the western chiefs; of Prince Meatha O'Faelan; of Dunlang O'Hartigan, beside whose litter walked Eevin of Craglea, her golden head sunk on her breast.

The warriors set down the litters and gathered silently and wearily about the corpse of King Brian Boru. They gazed unspeaking, their minds dulled from the agony of strife. Eevin lay motionless beside the body of her lover, as if she herself were dead; no tears stood in her eyes, no cry or moan escaped her pallid lips.

The clamor of battle was dying as the setting sun bathed the trampled field in its roseate light. The fugitives, tattered and slashed, were limping into the gates of Dublin, and the warriors of King Sitric were preparing to stand siege. But the Irish were in no condition to besiege the city. Four thousand warriors and chieftains had fallen, and nearly all the champions of the Gael were dead. But more than seven thousand Danes and Leinstermen lay stretched on the blood-soaked earth, and the power of the Vikings was broken. On Clontarf their iron reign was ended.

Conn walked toward the river, feeling now the ache of his stiffening wounds. He met Turlogh Dubh. The madness of battle was gone from Black Turlogh, and his dark face was inscrutable. From head to foot he was splattered with crimson.

"My Lord," said Conn, fingering the great copper

ring about his neck, "I have slain the man who put this thrall-mark on me. I would be free of it."

Black Turlogh took his red-stained ax-head in his hands and, pressing it against the ring, drove the keen edge through the softer metal. The ax gashed Conn's shoulder, but neither heeded.

"Now I am truly free," said Conn, flexing his mighty arms. "My heart is heavy for the chiefs who have fallen, but my mind is mazed with wonder and glory. When will ever such a battle be fought again? Truly, it was a feast of the ravens, a sea of slaughter ..."

His voice trailed off, and he stood like a statue, head flung back, eyes staring into the clouded heavens. The sun was sinking in a dark-ocean of scarlet. Great clouds rolled and tumbled, piled mountainously against the smoldering red of the sunset. A wind blew out of them, biting, cold, and, borne on the wind, etched shadowy against the clouds, a vague, gigantic form went flying, heard and wild locks streaming in the gale, cloak billowing out like great wings—speeding into the mysterious blue mists that pulsed and shimmered in the brooding North.

"Look up there—in the sky!" cried Conn. "The Grey Man! It is he! The Grey Man with the single terrible eye. I saw him in the mountains of Torka. I glimpsed him brooding on the walls of Dublin while the battle raged. I saw him looming above Prince Murrogh as he died. Look! He rides the wind and races among the tall clouds. He swindles. He fades into the void! He vanishes!"

"It is Odin, god of the sea-people," said Turlogh sombrely. "His children are broken, his altars crumble, and his worshippers fallen before the swords of the South. He flees the new gods and their children, and returns to the blue gulfs of the North which gave him birth. No more will helpless victims howl beneath the daggers of his priests— no more will he stalk the black clouds." He shook his head darkly. "The Grey God passes, and we too are passing, though we have conquered. The days of the twilight come on amain, and a strange feeling is upon me as of a waning age. What are we all, too, but ghosts waning into the night?"

And he went on into the dusk, leaving Conn to his freedom—from thralldom and cruelty, as both he and all the Gaels were now free of the shadow of the Grey God and his ruthless worshippers.

Howard's love of the barbaric was that of a civilized man—a nostalgia for a supposedly simpler age. Here he deals with a period even more primitive than his usual settings; it shares, though, the sense of doom-laden violence that pervades most of his work.

SPEAR AND FANG

A-æa crouched close to the cave mouth, watching Ga-nor with wondering eyes. Ga-nor's occupation interested her, as well as Ga-nor himself. As for Ga-nor, he was too occupied with his work to notice her. A torch stuck in a niche in the cave wall dimly illuminated the roomy cavern, and by its light Ga-nor was laboriously tracing figures on the wall. With a piece of flint he scratched the outline and then with a twig dipped in ocher paint completed the figure. The result was crude, but gave evidence of real artistic genius, struggling for expression.

It was a mammoth that he sought to depict, and little A-æa's eyes widened with wonder and admiration. Wonderful! What though the beast lacked a leg and had no tail? It was tribesmen, just struggling out of utter barbarism, who were the critics, and to them Ga-nor was a past master.

However, it was not to watch the reproduction of a mammoth that A-æa hid among the scanty bushes by Ga-nor's cave. The admiration for the painting was as nothing beside the look of positive adoration with which she favored the artist. Indeed, Ga-nor was not unpleasing to the eye. Tall he was, towering well over six feet, leanly built, with mighty shoulders and narrow hips, the build of a fighting man. Both his hands and his feet were long and slim; and his features, thrown into bold profile by the flickering torch-light, were intelligent, with a high, broad forehead, topped by a mane of sandy hair.

A-æa herself was very easy to look upon. Her hair, as well as her eyes, was black and fell about her slim shoulders in a rippling wave. No ocher tattooing tinted her cheek, for she was still unmated.

Both the girl and the youth were perfect specimens of the great Cro-Magnon race which came from no man knows where and announced and enforced their supremacy over beast and beast-man.

A-æa glanced about nervously. All ideas to the contrary, customs and taboos are much more narrow and vigorously enforced among savage peoples.

The more primitive a race, the more intolerant their customs. Vice and licentiousness may be the rule, but the appearance of vice is shunned and contemned. So if A-æa had been discovered, hiding near the cave of an unattached young man, denunciation as a shameless woman would have been her lot, and doubtless a public whipping.

To be proper, A-æa should have played the modest, demure maiden, perhaps skilfully arousing the young artist's interest without seeming to do so. Then, if the youth was pleased, would have followed public wooing by means of crude love-songs and music from reed pipes. Then barter with her parents and then—marriage. Or no wooing at all, if the lover was wealthy.

But little A-æa was herself a mark of progress. Covert glances had failed to attract the attention of the young man who seemed engrossed with his artistry, so she had taken to the unconventional way of spying upon him, in hopes of finding some way to win him.

Ga-nor turned from his completed work, stretched and glanced toward the cave mouth. Like a frightened rabbit, little A-æa ducked and darted away.

When Ga-nor emerged from the cave, he was puzzled by the sight of a small, slender footprint in the soft loam outside the cave.

A-æa walked primly toward her own cave, which was, with most of the others, at some distance from Ga-nor's cave. As she did so, she noticed a group of warriors talking excitedly in front of the chief's cave.

A mere girl might not intrude upon the councils of men, but such was A-æa's curiosity, that she dared a scolding by slipping nearer. She heard the words "footprint" and "gur-na" (man-ape).

The footprints of a gur-na had been found in the forest, not far from the caves.

"Gur-na" was a word of hatred and horror to the people of the caves, for the creatures whom the tribesmen called "gur-na", or man-apes, were the hairy monsters of another age, the brutish men of the Neandertal. More feared than mammoth or tiger, they had ruled the forests until the Cro-Magnon men had come and waged savage warfare against them. Of mighty power and little mind, savage, bestial and cannibalistic, they inspired the tribesmen with loathing and horror—a horror transmitted through the ages in tales of ogres and goblins, of werewolves and beast-men.

They were fewer and more cunning, then. No longer they rushed roaring to battle, but cunning and frightful, they slunk about the forests, the terror of all beasts, brooding in their brutish minds with hatred for the men who had driven them from the best hunting grounds.

And ever the Cro-Magnon men trailed them down and slaughtered them, until sullenly they had withdrawn far into the deep forests. But the fear of them remained with the tribesmen, and no woman went into the jungle alone.

Sometimes children went, and sometimes they returned not; and searchers found but signs of a ghastly feast, with tracks that were not the tracks of beasts, nor yet the tracks of men.

And so a hunting party would go forth and hunt the monster down. Sometimes it gave battle and was slain, and sometimes it fled before them and escaped into the depths of the forest, where they dared not follow. Once a hunting party, reckless with the chase, had pursued a fleeing gur-na into the deep forest and there, in a deep ravine, where overhanging limbs shut out the sunlight, numbers of the Neandertalers had come upon them.

So no more entered the forests.

A-æa turned away, with a glance at the forest. Somewhere in its depths lurked the beast-man, piggish eyes glinting crafty hate, malevolent, frightful.

Someone stepped across her path. It was Ka-nanu, the son of a councilor of the chief.

She drew away with a shrug of her shoulders. She did not like Ka-nanu and she was afraid of him. He wooed her with a mocking air, as if he did it merely for amusement and would take her whenever he wished, anyway. He seized her by the wrist.

"Turn not away, fair maiden," said he. "It is your slave, Ka-nanu."

"Let me go," she answered. "I must go to the spring for water."

"Then I will go with you, moon of delight, so that no beast may harm you."

And accompany her he did, in spite of her protests.

"There is a gur-na abroad," he told her sternly. "It is lawful for a man to accompany even an unmated maiden, for protection. And I am Ka-nanu," he added, in a different tone; "do not resist me too far, or I will teach you obedience."

A-æa knew somewhat of the man's ruthless nature. Many of the tribal girls looked with favor on Ka-nanu, for he was bigger and taller even than Ga-nor, and more handsome in a reckless, cruel way. But A-æa loved Ga-nor and she was afraid of

Ka-nanu. Her very fear of him kept her from resisting his approaches too much. Ga-nor was known to be gentle with women, if careless of them, while Ka-nanu, thereby showing himself to be another mark of progress, was proud of his success with women and used his power over them in no gentle fashion.

A-æa found Ka-nanu was to be feared more than a beast, for at the spring just out of sight of the caves, he seized her in his arms.

"A-æa," he whispered, "my little antelope, I have you at last. You shall not escape me."

In vain she struggled and pleaded with him. Lifting her in his mighty arms he strode away into the forest.

Frantically she strove to escape, to dissuade him.

"I am not powerful enough to resist you," she said, "but I will accuse you before the tribe."

"You will never accuse me, little antelope," he said, and she read another, even more sinister intention in his cruel countenance.

On and on into the forest he carried her, and in the midst of a glade he paused, his hunter's instinct alert.

From the trees in front of them dropped a hideous monster, a hairy, misshapen, frightful thing.

A-æa's scream re-echoed through the forest, as the thing approached. Ka-nanu, white-lipped and horrified, dropped A-æa to the ground and told her to run. Then, drawing knife and ax, he advanced.

The Neandertal man plunged forward on short, gnarled legs. He was covered with hair and his features were more hideous than an ape's because of the grotesque quality of the man in them. Flat, flaring nostrils, retreating chin, fangs, no forehead whatever, great, immensely long arms dangling from sloping, incredible shoulders, the monster seemed like the devil himself to the terrified girl. His apelike head came scarcely to Ka-nanu's shoulders, yet he must have outweighed the warrior by nearly a hundred pounds.

On he came like a charging buffalo, and Ka-nanu met him squarely and boldly. With flint ax and obsidian dagger he thrust and smote, but the ax was brushed aside like a toy and the arm that held the knife snapped like a stick in the misshapen hand of the Neandertaler. The girl saw the councilor's son wrenched from the ground and swung into the air, saw hum hurled clear across the glade, saw the monster leap after him and rend him limb from limb.

Then the Neandertaler turned his attention to her. A new expression came into his hideous eyes as he lumbered toward her, his great hairy hands horridly smeared with blood, reaching toward her.

Unable to flee, she lay dizzy with horror and fear. And the monster dragged her to him, leering into her eyes. He swung her over his shoulder and waddled away through the trees; and the girl, half-fainting, knew that he was taking her to his lair, where no man would dare come to rescue her.

Ga-nor came down to the spring to drink. Idly he noticed the faint footprints of a couple who had come before him. Idly he noticed that they had not returned.

Each footprint has its individual characteristic. That of the man he knew to be Ka-nanu. The other track was the same as that in front of his cave. He wondered, idly as Ga-nor was wont to do all things except the painting of pictures.

Then, at the spring, he noticed that the footprints of the girl ceased, but that the man's turned toward the jungle and were more deeply imprinted than before. Therefore Ka-nanu was carrying the girl.

Ga-nor was no fool. He knew that a man carries a girl into the forest for no good purpose. If she had been willing to go, she would not have been carried.

Now Ga-nor (another mark of progress) was inclined to meddle in things not pertaining to him. Perhaps another man would have shrugged his shoulders and gone his way, reflecting that it would not be well to interfere with a son of a councilor. But Ga-nor had few interests, and once his interest was roused he was inclined to see a thing through. Moreover, though not renowned as a fighter, he feared no man.

Therefore, he loosened ax and dagger in his belt, shifted his grip on his spear, and took up the trail.

On and on, deeper and deeper into the forest, the Neandertaler carried little A-æa.

The forest was silent and evil, no birds, no insects broke the stillness. Through the overhanging trees no sunlight filtered. On padded feet that made no noise the Neandertaler hurried on.

Beasts slunk out of his path. Once a great

python came slithering through the jungle and the Neandertaler took to the trees with surprising speed for one of his gigantic bulk. He was not at home in the trees, however, not even as much as A-æa would have been.

Once or twice the girl glimpsed another such monster as her captor. Evidently they had gone far beyond the vaguely defined boundaries of her race. The other Neandertal men avoided them. It was evident that they lived as do beasts, uniting only against some common enemy and not often then. Therein had lain the reason for the success of the Cro-Magnards' warfare against them.

Into a ravine he carried the girl, and into a cave, small and vaguely illumined by the light from without. He threw her roughly to the floor of the cave, where she lay, too terrified to rise.

The monster watched her, like some demon of the forest. He did not even jabber at her, as an ape would have done. The Neandertalers had no form of speech whatever

He offered her meat of some kind—uncooked, of course. Her mind reeling with horror, she saw that it was the arm of a Cro-Magnard child. When he saw she would not eat, he devoured it himself, tearing the flesh with great fangs.

He took her between his great hands, bruising her soft flesh. He ran rough fingers through her hair, and when he saw that he hurt her he seemed filled with a fiendish glee. He tore out handfuls of her hair, seeming to enjoy devilishly the torturing of his fair captive. A-æa set her teeth and would not scream as she had done at first, and presently he desisted.

The leopard-skin garment she wore seemed to enrage him. The leopard was his hereditary foe. He plucked it from her and tore it to pieces.

And meanwhile Ga-nor was hurrying through the forest. He was racing now, and his face was a devil's mask, for he had come upon the bloody glade and had found the monster's tracks leading away from it.

And in the cave in the ravine the Neandertaler reached for A-æa.

She sprang back and he plunged toward her. He had her in a corner but she slipped under his arm and sprang away. He was still between her and the outside of the cave.

Unless she could get past him, he would corner her and seize her. So she pretended to spring to one side. The Neandertaler lumbered in that direction, and quick as a cat she sprang the other way and darted past him, out into the ravine.

With a bellow he charged after her. A stone rolled beneath her foot, flinging her headlong; before she could rise his hand seized her shoulder. As he dragged her into the cave, she screamed, wildly, frenziedly, with no hope of rescue, just the scream of a woman in the grasp of a beast.

Ga-nor heard that scream as he bounded down into the ravine. He approached the cave swiftly but cautiously. As he looked in, he saw red rage. In the vague light of the cave, the great Neandertaler stood, his piggish eyes on his foe, hideous, hairy, blood-smeared, while at his feet, her soft white body contrasting with the shaggy monster, her long hair gripped in his blood-stained hand, lay A-æa.

The Neandertaler bellowed, dropped his captive and charged. And Ga-nor met him, not matching brute strength with his lesser might, but leaping back and out of the cave. His spear leaped and the monster bellowed as it tore through his arm. Leaping back again, the warrior jerked his spear and crouched. Again the Neandertaler rushed, and again the warrior leaped away and thrust, this time for the great hairy chest. And so they battled, speed and intelligence against brute strength and savagery.

Once the great, lashing arm of the monster caught Ga-nor upon the shoulder and hurled him a dozen feet away, rendering that arm nearly useless for a time. The Neandertaler bounded after him, but Ga-nor flung himself to one side and leaped to his feet. Again and again his spear drew blood, but it seemed only to enrage the monster.

Then before the warrior knew it, the wall of the ravine was at his back and he heard A-æa shriek as the monster rushed in. The spear was torn from his hand and he was in the grasp of his foe. The great arms encircled his neck and shoulders, the great fangs sought his throat. He thrust his elbow under the retreating chin of his antagonist, and with his free hand struck the hideous face again and again; blows that would have felled an ordinary man but which the Neandertal beast did not even notice.

Ga-nor felt consciousness going from him. The terrific arms were crushing him, threatening to break his neck. Over the shoulder of his foe he saw the girl approaching with a great stone, and he tried to motion her back.

With a great effort he reached down over the monster's arm and found his ax. But so close were they clinched together that he could not draw it. The Neandertal man set himself to break his foe to pieces as one breaks a stick. But Ga-nor's elbow was thrust under his chin, and the more the Neandertal man tugged, the deeper drove the elbow into his hairy throat. Presently he realized that fact and flung Ga-nor away from him. As he did so, the warrior drew his ax, and striking with the fury of desperation, clove the monster's head.

For a minute Ga-nor stood reeling above his foe, then he felt a soft form within his arms and saw a pretty face, close to his.

"Ga-nor!" A-æa whispered, and Ga-nor gathered the girl in his arms.

"What I have fought for I will keep," he said.

And so it was that the girl who went forth into the forest in the arms of an abductor came back in the arms of a lover and a mate.

If ever there was a real time and place that corresponded to Howard's wildly romantic imaginings, it was the fifth and sixth centuries AD, the age of the volkerwanderung when Rome went under and the Germanic tribes were on the move across Europe, Asia and North Africa. A figure like Genseric of the Vandals, born on the Danube and ending his life as the sacker of Rome, leading his people on horseback, wagon, and galley across thousands of miles, is strange and marvelous enough for any fantasy. He appears in this story with another legendary figure. . . .

DELENDA EST

"It's no empire, I tell you! It's only a sham. Empire? Pah! Pirates, that's all we are!" It was Hunegais, of course, the ever moody and gloomy, with his braided black locks and drooping moustaches betraying his Slavonic blood. He sighed gustily, and the Falernian wine slopped over the rim of the jade goblet clenched in his brawny hand, to stain his purple, gilt-embroidered tunic. He drank noisily, after the manner of a horse, and returned with melancholy gusto to his original complaint.

"What have we done in Africa? Destroyed the big landholders and the priests, set ourselves up as

landlords. Who works the land? Vandals? Not at all!
The same men who worked it under the Romans.
We've merely stepped into Roman shoes. We levy
taxes and rents, and are forced to defend the land
from the accursed Berbers. Our weakness is in our
numbers. We can't amalgamate with the people!
We'd be absorbed. We can't make allies and subjects
out of them; all we can do is maintain a sort of
military prestige—we are a small body of aliens sitting in castles and, for the present, enforcing our
rule over a big native population—who, it's true, hate
us no worse than they hated the Romans, but—"

"Some of that hate could be done away with,"
interrupted Athaulf. He was younger than Hunegais, clean shaven, and not unhandsome; his man-
ners were less primitive. He was a Suevi, whose
youth had been spent as a hostage in the East
Roman court. "They are orthodox; if we could
bring ourselves to renounce Arianism—"

"No!" Hunegais's heavy jaws came together with
a snap that would have splintered lesser teeth than
his. His dark eyes flamed with the fanaticism that
was, among all the Teutons, the exclusive possession
of his race. "Never! We are the masters! It is theirs
to submit—not ours. We *know* the truth of Arian;
if the miserable Africans can not realize their mistake, they must be made to see it—by torch and
sword and rack, if necessary!" Then his eyes dulled
again, and with another gusty sigh from the depths
of his belly, he groped for the wine jug.

"In a hundred years the Vandal kingdom will be
a memory," he predicted. "All that holds it
together now is the will of Genseric." He pro-
nounced it "Geiserich."

The individual so named laughed, leaned back in his carven ebony chair, and stretched out his muscular legs before him. Those were the legs of a horseman; but their owner had exchanged the saddle for the deck of a war galley. Within a generation, he had turned a race of horsemen into a race of searovers. He was the king of a race whose name had already become a term for destruction, and he was the possessor of the finest brain in the known world.

Born on the banks of the Danube and grown to manhood on that long trek westward, when the drifts of the nations crushed over the Roman palisades, he had brought to the crown forged for him in Spain all the wild wisdom the times could teach, in the feasting of swords and the surge and crush of races. His wild riders had swept the spears of the Roman rulers of Spain into oblivion. When the Visigoths and the Romans joined hands and began to look southward, it was the intrigues of Genseric which brought Attila's scarred Huns swarming westward, tusking the flaming horizons with their myriad lances. Attila was dead now, and none knew where lay his bones and his treasures, guarded by the ghosts of five hundred slaughtered slaves; his name thundered around the world, but in his day he had been but one of the pawns moved resistlessly by the hand of the Vandal king.

And when, after Chalons, the Gothic hosts moved down through the Pyrenées, Genseric had not waited to be crushed by superior numbers. Men still cursed the name of Boniface, who called on Genseric to aid him against his rival, Aetius, and opened the Vandal's road to Africa. His reconciliation with Rome had been too late, vain as the courage with which he had sought to undo what he had done. Boniface died on a Vandal spear, and a new kingdom rose in the south. And now Aetius, too, was dead, and the great war galleys of the Vandals were moving northward, the long oars dipping and flashing silver in the starlight, the great vessels heeling and rocking to the lift of the waves.

And in the cabin of the foremost galley, Genseric listened to the conversation of his captains, and smiled gently as he combed his unruly yellow beard with his muscular fingers. There was in his veins no trace of the Scythic blood which set his race somewhat aside from the other Teutons, from the long ago when scattered steppes-riders, drifting westward before the conquering Sarmatians, had come among the people dwelling on the upper reaches of the Elbe. Genseric was pure German; of medium height, with a magnificent sweep of shoulders and chest, and a massive corded neck, his frame promised as much of physical vitality as his wide blue eyes reflected mental vigor.

He was the strongest man in the known world, and he was a pirate—the first of the Teutonic sea-raiders whom men later called Vikings; but his domain of conquest was not the Baltic nor the blue North Sea, but the sunlit shores of the Mediterranean.

"And the will of Genseric," he laughed, in reply to Hunegais's last remark, "is that we drink and feast and let tomorrow take care of itself."

"So you say!" snorted Hunegais, with the freedom that still existed among the barbarians. "When did you ever let a tomorrow take care of itself? You plot and plot, not for tomorrow alone, but for a thousand tomorrows to come! You need not masquerade with us! We are not Romans to be fooled into thinking *you* are a fool—as Boniface was!"

"Aetius was no fool," muttered Thrasamund.

"But he's dead, and we are sailing on Rome," answered Hunegais, with the first sign of satisfaction he had yet evinced. "Alaric didn't get all the loot, thank God! And I'm glad Attila lost his nerve at the last minute—the more plunder for us."

"Attila remembered Chalons," drawled Athaulf. "There is something about Rome that lives—by the saints, it is strange. Even when the empire seems most ruined—torn, befouled, and tattered—some part of it springs into life again. Stilicho, Theodosius, Aetius—who can tell? Tonight in Rome there may be a man sleeping who will overthrow us all."

Hunegais snorted and hammered on the wine-stained board.

"Rome is as dead as the white mare I rode at the taking of Carthage! We have but to stretch out our hands and grasp the plunder of her!"

"There was a great general once who thought as much," said Thrasamund drowsily. "A Carthaginian, too, by God! I have forgotten his name. But he beat the Romans at every turn. Cut, slash, that was his way!"

"Well," remarked Hunegais, "he must have lost at last, or he would have destroyed Rome."

"That's so!" ejaculated Thrasamund.

"We are not Carthaginians," laughed Genseric. "And who said aught of plundering Rome? Are we not merely sailing to the imperial city in answer to the appeal of the Empress who is beset by jealous foes? And now, get out of here, all of you. I want to sleep."

The cabin door slammed on the morose predictions of Hunegais, the witty retorts of Athaulf, the mumble of the others. Genseric rose and moved over to the table, to pour himself a last glass of wine. He walked with a limp; a Frankish spear had girded him in the leg long years ago.

He lifted the jeweled goblet to his lips—wheeled with a startled oath. He had not heard the cabin door open, but a man was standing across the table from him.

"By Odin!" Genseric's Arianism was scarcely skin-deep. "What do you in my cabin?"

The voice was calm, almost placid, after the first startled oath. The king was too shrewd to often evince his real emotions. His hand stealthily closed on the hilt of his sword. A sudden and unexpected stroke—

But the man made no hostile movement. He was a stranger to Genseric, and the Vandal knew he was neither Teuton nor Roman. He was tall, dark, with a stately head, his flowing locks confined by a dark crimson band. A curling, patriarchal beard swept his breast. A dim, misplaced familiarity twitched at the Vandal's mind as he looked.

"I have not come to harm you!" The voice was deep, strong, and resonant. Genseric could tell little of his attire, since he was masked in a wide dark cloak. The Vandal wondered if he grasped a weapon under that cloak.

"Who are you, and how did you get into my cabin?" he demanded.

"Who I am, it matters not," returned the other. "I have been on this ship since you sailed from Carthage. You sailed at night; I came aboard then."

"I never saw you in Carthage," muttered Genseric.

"And you are a man who would stand out in a crowd."

"I dwell in Carthage," the stranger replied. "I have dwelt there for many years. I was born there, and my forefathers before me. Carthage is my life!" The last sentence was uttered in a voice so passionate and fierce that Genseric involuntarily stepped back, his eyes narrowing.

"The folk of the city have some cause of complaint against us," said he. "But the looting and destruction was not by my orders. Even then it was my intention to make Carthage my capital. If you suffered loss by the sack, why—"

"Not from your wolves," grimly answered the other. "Sack of the city? I have seen such a sack as not even you, barbarian, have dreamed of! They call you barbaric. I have seen what civilized Romans can do."

"Romans have not plundered Carthage in my memory," muttered Genseric, frowning in some perplexity.

"Poetic justice!" cried the stranger, his hand emerging from his cloak to strike down on the table. Genseric noted that the hand was muscular yet white, the hand of an aristocrat. "Roman greed and treachery destroyed Carthage, trade rebuilt her in another guise. Now you, barbarian, sail from her harbors to humble her conqueror! Is it any wonder that old dreams silver the cords of your ships and creep amidst the holds, and that forgotten ghosts burst their immemorial tombs to glide upon your decks?"

"Who said anything of humbling Rome?" uneasily

demanded Genseric. "I merely sail to arbitrate a dispute as to succession—"

"Pah!" Again the hand slammed down on the table. "If you knew what I know, you would sweep that accursed city clean of life before you turn your prows southward again. Even now, those you sail to aid plot your ruin—and a traitor is on board your ship!"

"What do you mean?" Still there was neither excitement nor passion in the Vandal's voice.

"Suppose I gave you proof that your most trusted companion and vassal plots your ruin with those to whose aid you lift your sails?"

"Give me that proof; then ask what you will," answered Genseric with a touch of grimness.

"Take this in token of faith!" The stranger rang a coin on the table and caught up a silken girdle which Genseric himself had carelessly thrown down.

"Follow me to the cabin of your counsellor and scribe, the handsomest man among the barbarians—"

"Athaulf?" In spite of himself, Genseric started. "I trust him beyond all others."

"Then you are not as wise as I deemed you," grimly answered the other. "The traitor within is to be feared more than the foe without. It was not the legions of Rome which conquered me—it was the traitors within my gates. Not alone in swords and ships does Rome deal, but with the souls of men. I have come from a far land to save your empire and your life. In return I ask but one thing: drench Rome in blood!"

For an instant the stranger stood transfigured, mighty arm lifted, fist clenched, dark eyes flashing fire. An aura of terrific power emanated from him, aweing even the wild Vandal. Then sweeping his purple cloak about him with a kingly gesture, the man stalked to the door and through it, despite Genseric's exclamation and effort to detain him.

Swearing in bewilderment, the king limped to the door, opened it, and glared out on the deck. A lamp burned on the poop. A reek of unwashed bodies came up from the hold where the weary rowers toiled at their oars. The rhythmic clack vied with a dwindling chorus from the ships which followed in a long ghostly line. The moon struck silver from the waves, shone white on the deck. A single warrior stood on guard outside Genseric's door, the moonlight sparkling on his crested golden helmet and Roman corselet. He lifted his javelin in salute.

"Where did he go?" demanded the king.

"Who, my lord?" inquired the warrior stupidly.

"The tall man, dolt," exclaimed Genseric impatiently. "The man in the purple cloak who just left my cabin."

"None has left your cabin since the lord Hunegais and the others went forth, my lord," replied the Vandal in bewilderment.

"Liar!" Genseric's sword was a ripple of silver in his hand as it slid from its sheath. The warrior paled and shrank back.

"As God is my witness, king," he swore, "no such man have I seen this night."

Genseric glared at him; the Vandal king was a judge of men and he knew this one was not lying. He felt a peculiar twitching of his scalp, and turning without a word, limped hurriedly to Athaulf's cabin. There he hesitated, then threw open the door.

Athaulf lay sprawled across a table in an attitude which needed no second glance to classify. His face was purple, his glassy eyes distended, and his tongue lolled out blackly. About his neck, knotted in such a knot as seamen make, was Genseric's silken girdle. Near one hand lay a quill, near the other, ink and a piece of parchment. Catching it up, Genseric read laboriously.

To her majesty, the empress of Rome:
I, thy faithful servant, have done thy bidding, and am prepared to persuade the barbarian I serve to delay his onset on the imperial city until the aid you expect from Byzantium has arrived. Then I will guide him into the bay I mentioned, where he can be caught as in a vise and destroyed with his whole fleet, and—

The writing ceased with an erratic scrawl. Genseric glared down at him, and again the short hairs lifted on his scalp. There was no sign of the tall stranger, and the Vandal knew he would never be seen again.

"Rome shall pay for this," he muttered. The mask he wore in public had fallen away; the Vandal's face was that of a hungry wolf. In his glare, in the knotting of his mighty hand, it took no sage to read the doom of Rome. He suddenly remembered that he still clutched in his hand the coin the stranger had dropped on his table. He glanced at it, and his breath hissed between his teeth, as he recognized the characters of an old, forgotten language, the features of a man which he had often seen carved in ancient marble in old Carthage, preserved from Roman hate.

"Hannibal!" muttered Genseric.

Another of Howard's techniques was the use of reincarnation or a narrator in touch with "racial memories" of distant times. "Marchers" starts with a rather awkward introduction of that sort, and continues in fine Howardian style as a band of proto-Nordic raiders cut their way across the world from Central Asia to Texas driven by sheer restlessness and bloodlust. Perhaps some of Howard's own frustration at being penned in the narrow lane of small-town ways shines through this story; and there is projection of himself in the crippled narrator who dreams of striding boldly, sword in hand, as the giant Hialmar.

MARCHERS OF VALHALLA

The sky was lurid, gloomy and repellent, of the blue of tarnished steel, streaked with dully crimson banners. Against the muddled red smear lowered the low hills that are the peaks of that barren upland which is a dreary expanse of sand drifts and post-oak thickets, checkered with sterile fields where tenant farmers toil out their hideously barren lives in fruitless labor and bitter want.

I had limped to a ridge which rose above the others, flanked on either hand by the dry post-oak thickets. The terrible dreariness of the grim desolation of the vistas spread before me turned my soul to dust and ashes. I sank down upon a half-rotted log, and the agonizing melancholy of that drab land lay hard upon me. The red sun, half veiled in blowing dust and filmy cloud, sank low; it hung a hand's breadth above the western rim. But its setting lent no glory to the sand drifts and shinnery. Its somber glow but accentuated the grisly desolation of the land.

Then suddenly I realized that I was not alone. A woman had come from the dense thicket, and stood looking down at me. I gazed at her in silent wonder. Beauty was so rare in my life I was hardly able to recognize it, yet I knew that this woman was unbelievably beautiful. She was neither short nor tall; slender and yet splendidly shaped. I do not remember her dress; I have a vague impression that she was richly but modestly clad. But I remember the strange beauty of her face, framed in the dark rippling glory of her hair. Her eyes held mine like a magnet; I can not tell you the color of those eyes. They were dark and luminous, lighted as no eyes I ever saw were lighted. She spoke and her voice, strangely accented, was alien to my ears, and golden as distant chimes.

"Why do you fret, Hialmar?"

"You mistake me, Miss," I answered. "My name is James Allison. Were you looking for someone?"

She shook her head slowly.

"I came to look at the land once more. I had not thought to find you here."

"I don't understand you," I said. "I never saw you before. Are you a native of this country? You don't talk like a Texan."

She shook her head.

"No. But I knew this land long ago—long, long ago."

"You don't look that old," I said bluntly. "You'll pardon me for not getting up. As you see, I have but one leg, and it was such a long walk up here that I'm forced to sit and rest."

"Life has dealt harshly with you," she said softly. "I had hardly recognized you. Your body is so changed—"

"You must have known me before I lost my leg," I said bitterly, "although I'll swear I can't remember you. I was only fourteen when a mustang fell on me and crushed my leg so badly it had to be amputated. I wish to God it had been my neck."

Thus cripples speak to utter strangers—not so much a bid for sympathy, but the despairing cry of a soul tortured beyond endurance.

"Do not fret," she said softly. "Life takes but it also gives—"

"Oh, don't give me a speech about resignation and cheerfulness!" I cried savagely. "If I had the power I'd strangle every damned blatant optimist in the world! What have I to be merry about? What have I to do except sit and wait for the death which is slowly creeping on me from an incurable malady? I have no memories to cheer me—no future to look forward to—except a few more years of pain and woe, and then the blackness of utter oblivion. There has not even been any beauty in my life, lying as it has in this forsaken and desolate wilderness."

The dams of my reticence were broken, and my bitter dreams, long pent up, burst forth; nor did it seem strange that I should pour out my soul to a strange woman I had never seen before.

"The country has memories," she said.

"Yes, but I have not shared in them. I could have loved life and lived deeply as a cowboy, even here, before the squatters turned the country from an open range to a drift of struggling farms. I could have lived deep as a buffalo hunter, an Indian fighter, or an explorer, even here. But I was born out of my time, and even the exploits of this weary age were denied me.

"It's bitter beyond human telling to sit chained and helpless, and feel the hot blood drying in my veins, and the glittering dreams fading in my brain. I come of a restless, roving, fighting race. My great-grandfather died at the Alamo, shoulder to shoulder with David Crockett. My grandfather rode with Jack Hayes and Bigfoot Wallace, and fell with three-quarters of Hood's brigade. My oldest brother fell at Vimy Ridge, fighting with the Canadians, and the other died at the Argonne. My father is a cripple, too; he sits drowsing in his chair all day, but his dreams are full of brave memories, for the bullet that broke his leg struck him as he charged up San Juan Hill.

"But what have I to feel or dream or think?"

"You should remember," she said softly. "Even now dreams should come to you like the echoes of distant lutes. I remember! How I crawled to you on my knees, and you spared me—aye, and the crashing and the thundering as the land gave way—man, do you never dream of drowning?"

I started.

"How could you know that? Time and again I

have felt the churning, seething waters rise like a
green mountain over me, and have wakened, gasping and strangling—but how could you know?"

"The bodies change; the soul remains slumber-
ing and untouched," she answered cryptically.
"Even the world changes. This is a dreary land,
you say, yet its memories are ancient and marvel-
lous beyond the memories of Egypt."

I shook my head in wonder.

"Either you're insane, or I am. Texas has glorious memories of war and conquest and drama—
but what are her few hundred years of history,
compared to the antiquities of Egypt—in
ancientness, I mean?"

"What is the peculiarity of the state as a whole?"
she asked.

"I don't know exactly what you mean," I
answered. "If you mean geologically, the peculiarity that has struck me is the fact that the land is
but a succession of broad tablelands, or shelves,
sloping upward from sea-level to over four thousand feet elevation, like the steps of a gigantic
stair, with breaks of timbered hills between. The
last break is the Caprock, and above that begins
the Great Plains."

"Once the Great Plains stretched to the Gulf,"
she said. "Long, long ago what is now the state of
Texas was a vast upland plateau, sloping gently to
the coast, but without the breaks and shelvings of
today. A mighty cataclysm broke off the land at
the Caprock, the ocean roared over it, and the
Caprock became the new shoreline. Then, age by
age, the waters slowly receded, leaving the steppes
as they are today. But in receding they swept into

the depths of the Gulf many curious things—man, do you not remember—the vast plains that ran from the sunset to the cliffs above the shining sea? And the great city that loomed above those cliffs?"

I stared at her, bewildered. Suddenly she leaned toward me, and the glory of her alien beauty almost overpowered me. My senses reeled. She threw her hands before my eyes with a strange gesture.

"You shall see!" she cried sharply. "You see— what do you see?"

"I see the sand drifts and the shinnery thickets gloomy with sunset," I answered like a man speaking slowly, in a trance. "I see the sun resting on the western horizon."

"You see vast plains stretching to shining cliffs!" she cried. "You see the spires and the golden dome of the city, shimmering in the sunset! You see—"

As if night had shut down suddenly, darkness came upon me, and unreality, in which the only thing that had existence was her voice, urgent, commanding—

There was a sense of fading time and space—a sensation of being whirled over illimitable gulfs, with cosmic winds blowing against me—then I looked upon churning clouds, unreal and luminous, which crystalized into a strange landscape— familiar, and yet fantastically unfamiliar. Vast treeless plains swept away to merge with hazy horizons. In the distance, to the south, a great black cyclopean city reared its spires against the evening sky, and beyond it shone the blue waters of a placid sea. And in the near distance a line of figures moved through the still expanse. They were big men, with yellow hair and cold blue eyes, clad in scale-mail corselets and horned helmets, and they bore shields and swords.

One differed from the rest in that he was short, though strongly made, and dark. And the tall yellow-haired warrior that walked beside him—for a fleeting instant there was a distinct sense of duality. I, James Allison of the twentieth century, saw and recognized the man who was I in that dim age and that strange land. This sensation faded almost instantly, and I was Hialmar, a son of the Fair-haired, without cognizance of any other existence, past or future.

Yet as I tell the tale of Hialmar, I should perforce interpret some of what he saw and did and was, not as Hialmar, but as the modern I. These interpretations you will recognize in their place. But remember Hialmar was Hialmar and not James Allison; that he knew no more and no less than was contained in his own experiences, bounded by the boundaries of his own life. I am James Allison and I was Hialmar, but Hialmar was not James Allison; man may look back for ten thousand years; he can not look forward, even for an instant.

We were five hundred men and our gaze was fixed on the black towers which reared against the blue of sea and sky. All day we had guided our course by them, since the first red glow of dawn had disclosed them to our wondering eyes. A man could see far across those level, grassy plains; at first sight we had thought that city near, but we had trudged all day, and still we were miles away.

Lurking in our minds had been the thought that it was a ghost city—one of the phantoms which had haunted us on our long march across the bitter dusty deserts to the west, where, in the burning skies we had seen mirrored, still lakes, bordered by palms, and winding rivers, and spacious cities, all which vanished as we approached. But this was no mirage, born of sun and dust and silence. Etched in the clear evening sky we saw plainly the giant details of massive turret and grim abutment; of serrated tower and titanic wall.

In what dim age did I, Hialmar, march with my tribesmen across those plains toward a nameless city? I can not say. It was so long ago that the yellow-haired folk still dwelt in Nordheim, and were called, not Aryans, but red-haired Vanir and golden-haired Æsir. It was before the great drifts of my race had peopled the world, yet lesser, nameless drifts, had already begun. We were the travelling of years from our northern homeland. Lands and seas lay between. Oh, that long, long trek! No drift of people, not even of my own people, whose drifts have been epic, has never equalled it. It had led us around the world—down from the snowy north into rolling plains, and mountain valleys tilled by peaceful brown folk— into hot breathless jungles, reeking with rot and teeming with spawning life—through eastern lands flaming with raw primitive colors under the waving palm-trees, where ancient races lived in cities of carven stone—up again into the ice and snow and across a frozen arm of the sea—then down through the snow-clad wastes, where squat blubber-eating men fled squalling from our swords; southward and eastward through gigantic mountains and titanic forest, lonely and gigantic and desolate as Eden, after man was cast forth—over searing desert sands and boundless plains, until at last, beyond the silent black city, we saw the sea once more.

Men had grown old on that trek. I, Hialmar, had come to manhood. When I had first set forth on the long trail, I had been a young boy; now I was a young man, a proven warrior, mighty limbed, with great broad shoulders, a corded throat, and an iron heart.

We were all mighty men—giants beyond the comprehension of moderns. There is not on earth today a man as strong as the weakest of our band, and our mighty thews were tuned to a blinding speed that would make the motions of finely-trained modern athletes seem stodgy and clumsy and slow. Our might was more than physical; born of a wolfish race, the years of our wandering and fighting man and beast and the elements in all forms, had instilled in our souls the very spirit of the wild—the intangible power that quivers in the long howl of the grey wolf, that roars in the north wind, that sleeps in the mighty unrest of turbulent rivers, that sounds in the slashing of icy sleet, the beat of the eagle's wings, and lurks in the brooding silence of the vast places.

I have said it was a strange trek. It was no drift of a whole tribe, men and yellow-haired women and naked children. We were all men, adventurers to whom even the ways of wandering, warlike folk

were too tame. We had taken the trail alone, conquering, exploring and wandering, driven only by
our paranoidal drive to see beyond the horizon.

There had been more than a thousand at the
beginning; now there were five hundred. The
bones of the rest bleached along that world-
circling trail. Many chiefs had led us and died. Now
our chief was Asgrimm, grown old on that endless
wandering—a gaunt, bitter fighter, one-eyed and
wolfish, who forever gnawed his greying beard.

We came of many clans, but all of the golden-
haired Æsir, except the man who strode beside
me. He was Kelka, my blood brother, and a Pict.
He had joined us among the jungle-clad hills of a
far land that marked the eastern-most drift of his
race, where the tom-toms of his people pulsed
incessantly through the hot star-flecked night. He
was short, thick-limbed, deadly as a jungle-cat. We
of the Æsir were barbarians, but Kelka was a savage. Behind him lay the abysmal chaos of the
squalling black jungle. The pad of the tiger was in
his stealthy tread, the grip of the gorilla in his
black-nailed hands; the fire that burns in a leopard's eyes burned in his.

Oh, we were a hard-bitten horde, and our tracks
had been laid in blood and smoldering embers in
many lands. I dare not repeat what slaughters, rapine and massacres lay behind us, for you would
recoil in horror. You are of a softer, milder age,
and you can not understand those savage times
when wolf pack tore wolf pack, and the morals
and standards of life differed from those of this
age as the thoughts of a grey killer wolf differ from
those of a fat lap-dog dozing before the hearth.

This long explanation I have given in order that you may understand what sort of men marched across that plain toward the city, and by this understanding interpret what came after. Without this understanding the saga of Hialmar is howling chaos, without rhyme or meaning.

As we looked at the great city we were not awed. We had ravaged red-handed through cities in other lands beyond the sea. Many conflicts had taught us to avoid battle with superior forces when possible, but we had no fear. We were equally ready for war or the feast of friendship, as the people of the city might choose.

They had seen us. We were close enough to make out the lines of orchards, fields and vineyards outside the walls, and the figures of the workers scurrying to the city. We saw the glitter of spears on the battlements, and heard the quick throb of war-drums.

"It will be war, brother," said Kelka gutturally, setting his bucket firmly on his left arm. We took up our girdles and gripped our weapons—not of copper and bronze as our people in far Nordheim still worked in, but of keen steel, fashioned by a conquered, cunning people in the land of palm-trees and elephants, whose steel-armed warriors had not been able to withstand us.

We drew up on the plain a moderate distance from the great black walls, which seemed to be built of gigantic blocks of basaltic stone. From our lines Asgrimm strode, weaponless, with his hands lifted, open palm outward, as a sign of parley. But an arrow cut into the sod near him, arching from the turrets, and he fell back to our lines.

"War, brother!" hissed Kelka, red fires glimmering in his black eyes. And at that instant the mighty gates swung open, and out filed lines of warriors, their war-plumes nodding above them in a glitter of lifted spears. The westering sun striking fire from their burnished copper helmets.

They were tall and leanly built, dark of skin, though neither brown nor black, with straight hawk-like features. Their harness was of copper and leather, their bucklers covered with glossy shagreen. Their spears and slender swords and long daggers were of bronze. They advanced in perfect formation, fifteen hundred strong, a surging tide of nodding plumes and gleaming spears. The battlements behind them were lined with watchers.

There was no parley. As they came, old Asgrimm gave tongue like a hunting wolf and we charged to meet the attack. We had no formation; we ran toward them like wolves, and we saw scorn in their hawk-features as we neared them. They had no bows, and not an arrow was winged from our racing lines, not a spear thrown. We wished only to come to hand-grips. When we were within javelin-cast they sent a shower of spears, most of which glanced from our shields and corselets, and then with a deep-throated roar, our charge crashed home.

Who said the ordered discipline of a degenerate civilization can match the sheer ferocity of barbarism? They strove to fight as a unit; we fought as individuals, rushing headlong against their spears, hacking like mad men. Their entire first rank went down beneath our whistling swords, and the ranks behind crushed back and wavered as the warriors felt the brute impact of our incredible strength. If they had held, they might have flanked us, hemmed us in with their superior numbers, and slaughtered us. But they could not stand. In a storm of hammering swords we ploughed through, breaking their lines, treading their dead underfoot as we surged irresistibly onward. Their battle formation melted; they strove against us, man to man, and the battle became a slaughter. For in personal strength and ferocity, they were not match for us.

We hewed them down like corn; we reaped them like ripe grain! Oh, when I relive that battle, it seems that James Allison gives place to the mailed and mighty Hialmar, with the war-madness in his brain and the war-chant on his lips! And I am drunken again with the singing of the swords, the spattering of hot blood, and the roar of the slaying.

They broke and fled, casting away their spears. We were hard at their heels, cutting them down us they ran, to the very gates through which the foremost streamed and which they slammed in our faces, and in the faces of the wretches who were last in the flight. Shut off from safety these clawed and yammered at the unyielding portals until we hewed them down. Then we, in turn, battered at the gates until a shower of stones and beams cast from above, brained three of our warriors, and we gave back to a safe distance. We heard the women howling in the streets, and the men lined the walls and shot arrows at us, with no great skill.

The bodies of the slain strewed the plain from the spot where the hosts clashed to the threshold of the gates, and where one Æsir had died, half a dozen plumed warriors had fallen.

The sun had set. We pitched our rude camp before the gates, and all night we heard wailing and moaning within the walls, where the people howled for those whose still bodies we plundered and cast in a heap some distance away. At dawn we took the corpses of the thirty Æsir who had fallen in the fight, and leaving archers to watch the city, we bore them to the cliffs, which pitched sheer for fifteen hundred feet to the white sandy beach. We found sloping defiles which led down, and made our way to the water's edge with our burdens.

There, from fishing boats drawn up on the sands, we fashioned a great raft, and heaped it high with driftwood. On the pile we laid the dead warriors, clad in their mail, with their weapons by their sides, and we cut the throats of the dozen captives we had taken, and stained the weapons and the raft-sides with their blood. Then we set the torch to the wood, and shoved the raft off. It floated far out on the mirrored surface of the blue water, until it was but a red glare, fading into the rising dawn.

Then we went back up the defiles, and ranged ourselves before the city, chanting our war-songs. We unslung our bows, and man after man toppled from the turrets, pierced by our long shafts. From trees we found growing in the gardens outside the city, we built scaling ladders, and set them against the walls. We swarmed up them in the teeth of arrow and spear and falling beam. They poured molten lead down on us, and burnt four warriors like ants in a flame. Then once more we plied our shafts, until no plumed heads showed on the battlements.

Under cover of our archers, we again set up the ladders. As we tensed ourselves for the upward rush that would carry us over the walls, on one of the towers that rose above the gates appeared a figure which halted us in our tracks.

It was a woman, such as we had not seen for long years—golden hair blowing free in the wind, milky white skin gleaming in the sunlight. She called to us in our own tongue, stumblingly, as if she had not used the language in many years.

"Wait! My masters have a word for you."

"Masters!" Asgrimm spat the word. "Whom does a woman of the Æsir call masters, except the men of her own clan?"

She did not seem to understand, but she answered, "This is the city of Khemu, and the masters of Khemu are lords of this land. They bid me say to you that they can not stand before you in battle, but they say you shall have small profit if you scale the walls, because they will cut down their women and children with their own hands, and set fire to the palaces, so you will take only a mass of crumbling stones. But if you will spare the city, they will send out to you presents of gold and jewels, rich wines and rare foods, and the fairest girls of the city."

Asgrimm tugged his beard, loath to forego the sacking and the blood-letting; but the younger men roared: "Spare the city, old grizzly! Otherwise they will kill the women—and we have wandered many a moon where no women came."

"Young fools!" snarled Asgrimm. "The kisses and love-cries of women fade and pall, but the sword sings a fresh song with each stroke. Is it the false lure of women, or the bright madness of slaughter?"

"Women!" roared the young warriors, clashing their swords. "Let them send out their girls, and we will spare their cursed city."

Old Asgrimm turned with a sneer of bitter scorn, and called to the golden-haired girl on the tower.

"I would raze your walls and spires into dust, and drench the dust with the blood of your masters," he said, "but my young men are fools! Send us forth food and women—and send us the sons of the chiefs for hostages."

"It shall be done, my lord," replied the girl, and we cast down the scaling ladders and retired to our camp.

Soon then the gates swung open again, and out filed a procession of naked slaves, laden with golden vessels containing foods and wines such as we had not known existed. They were directed by a hawk-faced man in a mantle of bright-hued feathers, bearing an ivory wand in his hand, and wearing on his temples a circlet of copper like a coiling serpent, the head reared up in front. It was evident from his bearing that he was a priest, and he spoke the name, Shakkaru, indicating himself. With him came half a dozen youths, clad in silken breeks, jeweled girdles and gay feathers, and trembling with fear. The yellow-haired girl stood on the tower and called to us that these were the sons of princes, and Asgrimm made them taste the wine and food before we ate or drank.

For Asgrimm the slaves brought amber jars filled with gold dust, a cloak of flaming crimson silk, a shagreen belt with a jewelled golden buckle, and a burnished copper head-dress adorned with great plumes.

He shook his head and muttered, "Gauds and bright trappings are dust of vanity and fade before the march of the years, but the edge of slaughter is not dulled, and the scent of fresh-spilled blood is good to an old man's nostrils."

But he donned the gleaming apparels, and then the girls came forth—slender young things, lithe and dark-eyed, scantily clad in shimmering silk— he chose the most beautiful, though morosely, as a man might pluck a bitter fruit.

Many a moon had passed since we had seen women, save the swart, smoke-stained creatures of the blubber-eaters. The warriors seized the terrified girls in fierce hunger—but my soul was dizzy with the sight of the golden-haired girl on the tower. In my mind there was room for no other thought. Asgrimm set me to guard the hostages, and to cut them down without mercy if the wine or food proved poisoned, or any woman stabbed a warrior with a hidden dagger, or the men of the city made a sudden sally on us.

But men came forth only to collect the bodies of their dead, which they burned, with many weird rituals, on a lofty promontory overlooking the sea.

Then there came to us another procession, longer and more elaborate than the first. Chiefs of the fighting men walked along unarmed, their harness exchanged for silken tunics and cloaks. Before them came Shakkaru, his ivory wand uplifted, and between the lines young slave youths, clad only in short mantles of parrot feathers, bore a canopied litter of polished mahogany, crusted with jewels.

Within sat a lean man with a curious crown on his high, narrow head. Beside the litter walked the white-skinned girl who had spoken from the tower. They came before us, and the slaves knelt, still supporting the litter, while the nobles gave back to each side, dropping to their knees. Only Shakkaru and the girl stood upright.

Old Asgrimm faced them, gaunt, fierce, wary, his deep-lined face shadowed by the black plumes which waved above it. And I thought how much more the natural king he looked, standing on his feet among his giant fighting men, sword in hand, than the man who lolled supinely in the slave-borne litter.

But my eyes were all for the girl, whom I saw for the first time face to face. She was clad only in a short, sleeveless and low-necked tunic of blue silk, which came to a hand's breath above her knees, and soft green leather sandals were on her feet. Her eyes were wide and clear, her skin whiter than the purest milk, and her hair caught the sun in a sheen of rippling gold. There was a softness about her slender form that I had never seen in any woman of the Æsir. There was a fierce beauty about our flaxen-haired women, but this girl was equally beautiful without that fierceness. She had not grown up in a naked land, as they had, where life was a merciless battle for existence, for man and for woman. But these thoughts I did not pursue to their last analysis; I merely stood, dazzled by the blond radiance of her, as she translated the words of the king, and the deep-growled replies of Asgrimm.

"My lord says to you, 'Lo, I am Akkheba, priest of Ishtar, king of Khemu. Let there be friendship between us. We have need of each other, for ye be men wandering blindly in a naked land, as my sorcery tells me, and the city of Khemu has need of keen swords and mighty arms, for a foe comes up against us out of the sea whom we can not withstand alone. Abide in this land, and lend your swords to us, and take our gifts for your pleasure and our girls for your wives. Our slaves shall toil for you, and each day you shall sit ye down at boards groaning with meats, fishes, grains, white breads, fruits and wines. Fine raiment shall you wear, and you shall dwell in marble palaces with silken couches and tinkling fountains.'"

Now Asgrimm understood this speech, for we had seen the cities of the palm-tree lands; but it was at the talk of foes and sword-heaving that his cold blue eyes gleamed.

"We will bide," he answered, and we roared our assent. "We will bide and cut out the hearts of the foes who come against you. But we will camp outside the walls, and the hostages will abide with us, night and day."

"It is well," said Akkheba, with a stately inclination of his narrow head, and the nobles of Khemu knelt before Asgrimm and would have kissed his high-strapped sandals. But he swore at them and gave back in wrathful embarrassment, while his warriors roared with rough mirth. Then Akkheba went back in his litter, bobbing on the shoulders of the slaves, and we settled ourselves for a long rest from our wanderings. My gaze hung on the golden-haired interpreter, until the gates of the city closed behind her.

So we dwelt outside the walls, and day by day the people brought us food and wine, and more girls were sent out to us. The workers came and toiled in the gardens, the fields and the vineyards without fear of us, and the fishing boats went out—narrow crafts with curving bows and striped silken sails. And we accepted the king's invitation at last, and went in a compact body, the hostages in the center with naked swords at their throats, through the iron-grilled gates and into the city.

By Ymir, Khemu was mightily built! Surely the present masters of the city sprang from the loins of gods, for who else could have reared up those black basaltic walls, eighty feet in height, and forty feet at the base? Or erected that great golden dome which rose five hundred feet above the marble-paved streets?

As we strode down the broad column-flanked street, and into the broad market place, our swords in our fists, doors and windows were crowded by eager faces, fascinated and frightened. The chatter of the market place died suddenly as we swung into it, and the people crowded back from the shops and stalls to give us room. We were wary as tigers, and the slightest mishap would have sufficed to make us explode in a frenzied burst of slaughter. But the people of Khemu were wise, and the provocation did not come.

The priests came and bowed before us and led us to the great palace of the king, a colossal pile of black stone and marble. Beside the palace was a broad, open court, paved with marble flags, and from this court marble steps, broad enough for ten men to mount abreast, led up to a dais, where the king stood on occasion to harangue the multitude. One wing of the palace extended behind this court, and against this wing the steps were built. This wing was of older construction than the rest of the palace, and was furnished with a curiously carven slanting roof of stone, steep and high, towering above all other spires in the city except the golden dome. The edge of this carven slope of masonry was but a few feet above the dais, and what was contained in that wing, none of the AEsir ever saw; folk said it was Akkheba's seraglio.

Beyond this open court were the mysterious column-fronted stone houses of the lesser priests, on both sides of a broad, marble-paved street, and beyond them again the lofty golden dome which crowned the great temple of Ishtar. On all sides rose sapphirean spires and gleaming towers, but the dome shone serenely above all, just as the bright glory of Ishtar, Shakkaru told us, shone above the heads of men. I say Shakkaru told us; in the few days they had spent among us, the young princes had learned much of our rugged, simple language, and by their interpretation and by the medium of signs, the priests of Khemu talked with us.

They led us to the lofty portals of the temple, but looking through the lines of tall marble columns, into the mysterious dim gloom of the interior, we balked, fearing a trap, and refused to go in. All the time I was looking eagerly for the golden-haired girl, but she was not in evidence. No longer needed as interpreter, the silence of the mysterious city had engulfed her.

After this first visit, we returned to our camp outside the walls, but we came again and again, at first in bands, and then, as our suspicions were lulled, in small groups or singly. However, we would not sleep within the city, though Akkheba urged us to pitch our tents in the great market place, if we disliked the marble palaces he offered us. No man of us had ever lived in a stone house, or within high walls. Our race dwelt in tents of tanned hides, or huts of mud and wattle, and we of the long trek as often as not slept like wolves on the naked earth. But by day we wandered through the city, marveling at the wonders of it, taking what we wished at the stalls, to the despair of the merchants, and entering palaces, warily, but at will, to be entertained by women who feared us, yet seemed to be fascinated by us. The people of Khemu were wondrous apt at learning; they soon spoke our language as well as we, though their speech came hard to our barbaric tongues.

But all this came in time. The day after we first visited the city, a number of us went again, and Shakkaru guided us to the palace of the higher priests which adjoined the temple of Ishtar. As we entered I saw the golden-haired girl, shining a pudgy copper idol with a handful of silk. Asgrimm laid a heavy hand on the shoulder of one of the young princes.

"Tell the priest that I would have that girl for

my own," he growled, but before the priest could reply, red rage rose in my brain and I stepped toward Asgrimm as a tiger steps toward his rival.

"If any man of us takes that woman it shall be Hialmar," I growled, and Asgrimm wheeled cat-like at the thick killer's purr in my voice. We faced each other tensely, our hands on our hilts, and Kelka grinned wolfishly and began to edge toward Asgrimm's back, stealthily drawing his long knife, when Akkheba spoke through the hostage.

"Nay, my lords, Aluna is not for either of you, or for any other man. She is handmaiden to the goddess Ishtar. Ask for any other woman in the city, and she shall be yours, even to the favorite of the king; but this woman is sacred to the goddess."

Asgrimm grunted and did not press the matter. The incense-breathing mystery of the temple had impressed even his fierce soul, and though we of the Æsir had not overmuch regard for other people's gods, yet he had no desire to take a girl who had been in such close communion with deity. But my superstitions were less than my desire for the girl Aluna. I came again and again to the palace of the priests, and though they little liked my coming, they would not, or dared not, say me nay; and with small beginnings, I did my wooing.

What shall I say of my skill at courtship? Another woman I might have dragged to my tent by her long hair, but even without the priestly ban, there was something in my regard for Aluna that tied my hands from violence. I wooed her in the way we of the Æsir wooed our fierce little beauties—with boastings of prowess, and tales of slaughter and rapine. And in truth, without exaggeration,

my tales of battle and massacre might have drawn
to me the most wayward of the fierce beauties of
Nordheim. But Aluna was soft and mild, and had
grown up in temple and palace, instead of wattle
hut and ice field! My ferocious boastings frightened her; she did not understand. And by the
strange perversity of nature, it was this very lack
of understanding which made her more enthralling
to me. Even as the very savagery she feared in me
made her look upon me with more interest than
she looked on the soft-thewed men of Khemu.

But in my conversations with her, I learned of
her coming to Khemu, and her saga was strange
as that of Asgrimm and our band. Where she had
dwelt in her childhood she could little say, having
no geography, but it had been far away across the
sea to the east. She remembered a bleak wave-
lashed coast, and straggling huts of wattle and
mud, and yellow-haired people like herself. So I
believe she came of a branch of the Æsir which
marked the westernmost drift of our race up to
that time. She was perhaps nine or ten years old
when she had been taken in a raid on the village
by dark-skinned men in galleys—who they were
she did not know, and my knowledge of ancient
times does not tell me, for then the Phoenicians
had not yet put to sea, nor the Egyptians. I can
but guess that they were men of some ancient
race, a survival of another age, like the people of
Khemu—destroyed and forgotten before the rise
of the younger races.

They took her, and a storm drove them westward and southward for many days, until their galley crashed on the reefs of a strange island where

alien, painted men swarmed onto the beach and slaughtered the survivors for their cooking pots. The yellow-haired child they spared, for some whim, and placing her in a great canoe with skulls grinning along the gunwales, they rowed until they sighted the spires of Khemu on the high cliffs.

There they sold her to the priests of Khemu, to be an handmaiden for the goddess Ishtar. I had supposed her position to be holy and revered, but I found that it was otherwise. The worm of suspicion stirred in my soul against the Khemuri, as I realized, in her words, the cruel and bitter contempt in which they held folk of other, younger races.

Her position in the temple was neither honorable nor dignified, and though the servant of the goddess, she was without honor herself, save that no man except the priests was allowed to touch her. She was, in fact, no more than a menial, subject to the cold cruelty of the hawk-like priests. She was not beautiful to them; to them her fair skin and shimmering golden hair were but the marks of an inferior race. And even to me, who was not prone to tax my brain, came the vague thought that if a blond girl was so contemptible in their eyes, that treachery must lurk behind the honor they gave to men of the same race.

Of Khemu I learned a little from Aluna and more from the priests and the princes. As a people, they were very old. They claimed descent from the half-mythical Lemurians. Once their cities had girdled the gulf upon which Khemu overlooked. But some the sea had gulped down, some had fallen before the painted savages of the islands, and some had been destroyed by civil wars, so that now, for near a thousand years, Khemu had reigned alone in solitary majesty. Their only contact had been with the wayward, painted people of the islands, who, until a year or so before, had come regularly in their long, high-prowed canoes to trade ambergris, coconuts, whale's teeth, and coral gotten from among their islands; and mahogany, leopard-skins, virgin gold, elephant tusks, and copper ore, procured from some unknown tropical mainland far to the south.

The people of Khemu were a waning race. Although they still numbered thousands, many were slaves, descendants of a thousand generations of slaves. Their race was but a shadow of its former greatness. A few more centuries would have seen the last of them, but on the sea to the south, out of sight over the horizon, was brooding a menace that threatened to sweep them all out of existence at one stroke.

The painted people had ceased to come in peaceful trade. They had come in war-canoes, with a clashing of spears on hide-covered shields, and a barbaric chant of war. A king had risen among them who had united the warring tribes, and now launched them against Khemu—not their former masters, for the old empire of which Khemu had been a part had crumbled before the drift of these people into the isles from that far-away continent which was the cradle of their race. This king was unlike them; he was a white-skinned giant like ourselves, with mad blue eyes and hair crimson as blood.

They had seen him, the people of Khemu. By

night his war-canoes full of painted spearmen had
stolen along the coast, and at sunrise the slayers
had swept up the defiles of the cliff, slaying the
fishermen who then slept in huts along the beach,
cutting down the laborers just going to work in
the fields, and storming at the gates. The great
walls had held, however, and the attackers had
despaired of the storming and drawn off. But the
red-haired king had stood up before the gates,
dangling the severed head of a woman by its long
hair, and shouted his bloody vow to return with a
fleet of war-canoes that should blacken the sea,
and to raze the towers of Khemu to the red-
stained dust. He and his slayers were the foes we
had been hired to fight, and we awaited their coming with fierce impatience.

And while we waited we grew more and more
used to the ways of civilization, insofar as barbarians can accustom themselves in such a short time.
We still camped outside the walls, and kept our
swords ready within, but it was more in instinctive
caution than fear of treachery. Even Asgrimm
seemed lulled to a sense of security, especially
after Kelka, maddened by the wine they gave him,
killed three Khemurians in the market-place, and
no blood-vengeance or man-bote for the deed.

We overcame our superstitions and allowed the
priests to guide us into the breathless dim cavern of
a building that was the temple of Ishtar. We went
even into the inner shrine, where sacred fires burned
dimly in the scented gloom. There a screaming slave
girl was sacrificed on the great black, red-veined altar
at the foot of the marble stairs which mounted
upward in the darkness until they were lost to view.

These stairs led to the abode of Ishtar, we were told, and up them the spirit of the sacrifice mounted to serve the goddess. Which I decided was true, for after the corpse on the altar lay still, and the chants of worship died to a blood-freezing whisper, I heard the sound of weeping far above us, and knew that the naked soul of the victim stood whimpering in terror before her goddess.

I asked Aluna later if she had ever seen the goddess, and she shook with fright, and said only the spirit of the dead looked on Ishtar. She, Aluna, had never set foot on the marble stair that led up to the abode of the goddess. She was called the hand-maiden of Ishtar, but her duties were to do the biddings of the hawk-faced priests and the evil-eyed naked women who served them, and who glided like dusky shadows among the purple gloom amidst the columns.

But among the warriors grew discontent, and they wearied of ease and luxury, and even of the dark-skinned women. For in the strange soul of the Æsir, only the lust for red battle and far-wandering remains constant. Asgrimm daily conversed with Shakkaru and Akkheba on ancient times; I was chained by the lure of Aluna; Kelka guzzled each day in the wine shops until he fell senseless in the streets. But the rest clamored against the life we were leading and asked Akkheba what of the foe we were to slay?

"Be patient," said Akkheba. "They will come, and their red-haired king with them."

Dawn rose over the shimmering spires of Khemu. Warriors had begun to spend the nights

as well as the days in the city. I had drunk with
Kelka the night before and lain with him in the
streets until the breeze of morn had blown the
fumes of the wine from my brain. Seeking Aluna,
I strode down the marble pave and entered the
palace of Shakkaru, which adjoined the temple of
Ishtar. I passed through the wide outer chambers,
where priests and women still lolled in slumber,
and heard on a sudden, beyond a closed door, the
sound of sharp blows on soft naked flesh. Mingled
with them was a piteous weeping and sobs for
mercy in a voice I knew.

The door was bolted, and it was of silver-braced
mahogany, but I burst it inwards as if it had been
match-wood. Aluna grovelled on the floor with her
scanty tunic tucked up, before a hatchet-faced
priest who with cold venom was scourging her
with a cruel, small-thonged whip which left crimson weals on her bare flesh. He turned as I
entered, and his face went ashy. Before he could
move I clenched my fist and gave him a buffet
that crushed his skull like an egg shell and broke
his neck in the bargain.

The whole palace swam red to my maddened
glare. Perhaps it was not so much the pain the
priest had inflicted on Aluna—because pain was
the most common thing in that fierce life—but
the proprietorial way in which he inflicted it—the
knowledge that the priests had possessed her—all
of them, perhaps.

A man is no better and no worse than his feel-
ings regarding the women of his blood, which is
the true and only test of racial consciousness. A
man will take to himself the stranger woman, and

sit down at meat with the stranger man, and feel no twinges of race-consciousness. It is only when he sees the alien man in possession of, or intent upon, a woman of his blood, that he realizes the difference in race and strain. So I, who had held women of many races in my arms, who was blood-brother to a Pictish savage, was shaken by mad fury at the sight of an alien laying hands on a woman of the Æsir.

I believe it was the sight of her, a slave of an alien race, and the slow wrath it produced, which first stirred me toward her. For the roots of love are set in hate and fury. And her unfamiliar softness and gentleness crystallized the first vague sensation.

Now I stood scowling down at her as she whimpered at my feet. I did not lift her and wipe her tears as a civilized man would have done. Had such a thought occurred to me, I would have rejected it disgustedly as unmanly.

As I stood so, I heard my name shouted suddenly, and Kelka raced into the chamber, yelling: "They come, brother, just as the old one said! The watchers on the cliffs have run to the city, with a tale of the sea black with war-boats!"

With a glance at Aluna, and a dumb incoherence struggling for expression, I turned to go with the Pict, but the girl staggered up and ran toward me, tears streaming down her cheeks, her arms outstretched pleadingly.

"Hialmar!" she wailed. "Do not leave me! I am afraid! I am afraid!"

"I can not take you now," I growled. "War and slaughter are forward. But when I return I will take you, and not the priests of all the gods shall stay me!"

I took a quick step toward her, my hands yearning toward her—then smitten with the fear of bruising her tender flesh, my hands dropped empty to my side. An instant I stood, dumb, torn by fierce yearning, speech and action frozen by the strangeness of the emotion which tore my soul. Then tearing myself away, I followed the impatient Pict into the streets.

The sun was rising as we of the Æsir marched toward the crimson-etched cliffs, followed by the regiments of Khemu. We had thrown aside the gay garments and head-pieces we had worn in the city. The rising sun sparkled on our horned helmets, worn hauberks and naked swords. Forgotten the months of idleness and debauchery. Our souls were riot with the wild exultation of coming strife. We went to slaughter as to a feast, and as we strode we clashed sword and shield in crude thundering rhythm, and sang the slaying-song of Niord who ate the red smoking heart of Heimdul. The warriors of Khemu looked at us in amazement, and the people who lined the walls of the city shook their heads in bewilderment and whispered among themselves.

So we came to the cliffs, and saw, as Kelka had said, the sea black with war-canoes, high prowed, and adorned with grinning skulls. Scores of these boats were already pulled up on the beach, and others were sweeping in on the crests of the waves. Warriors were dancing and shouting on the sands, and their clamor came up to us. There were many of them—three thousand, at the very least—

probably many more. The men of Khemu blenched, but old Asgrimm laughed as we had not heard him laugh in many a moon, and his age fell from him like a cast-off mantle.

There were half a dozen runways leading down through the cliffs to the beach, and up these the invaders must come, for the precipices on all other sides were unclimbable. We ranged ourselves at the heads of these runways, and the men of Khemu were behind us. Little part they had in that battle, holding themselves in reserve for aid that we did not call for.

Up the passes swarmed the chanting, painted warriors, and at last we saw their king, towering above the huge figures. The morning sun caught his hair in a crimson blaze, and his laughter was like a gust of sea wind. Alone of that horde he wore mail and helmet, and in his hand his great sword shone like a sheen of silver. Aye, he was one of the wandering Vanir, our red-haired kin in Nordheim. Of his long trek, his wanderings, and his wild saga, I know not, but that saga must have been wilder and stranger than that of Aluna's or of ours. By what madness in his soul he came to be king of these fierce savages, I can not even offer a guess. But when he saw what manner of men confronted him, new fury entered his yells, and at his bellow his warriors rolled up the runways like steel-crested waves.

We bent our bows and our arrows whistled in clouds down the defiles. The front ranks melted away, the hordes reeled backward, then stiffened and came on once more. Charge after charge we broke, and charge after charge hurtled up the passes in blind ferocity. The attackers wore no armor, and our long shafts tore through hide-covered shields like they were cloth. They had no skill at archery. When they came near enough they threw their spears in whistling showers, and some of us died. But few of them came within spear-cast and less won through to the heads of the passes. I remember one huge warrior who came crawling up out of the defile like a snake, crimson froth drooling from his lips, and the feathered ends of arrows standing out from his belly, ribs, neck and limbs. He howled like a mad dog, and his death-bite tore the heel of my sandal as I stamped his head into a red ruin.

Some few did break through the blinding hail and came to hand-grips, but there they fared little better. Man to man we of the Æsir were the stronger, and our armor turned their spears, while our swords and axes crashed through their wooden shields as though they were paper. Yet so many there were, but for our advantage in location, all the Æsir had died there on the cliffs, and the setting sun had lighted the smoking ruins of Khemu.

All through that long summer day we held the cliffs, until, when our quivers were empty and our bow-strings frayed through, and the defiles were choked with painted bodies, we threw aside our bows, and drawing our swords, went down into the defiles and met the invaders hand to hand and blade to blade. They had died like flies in the passes, yet there were many of them left, and the fire of their rage burned no less brightly because of the arrow-feathered corpses which lay beneath our feet.

They came on and up, roaring like a wave, stabbing with spear and lashing with war-club. We met them in a whirlwind of steel, cleaving skulls, smashing breasts, hewing limbs from their bodies and heads from their shoulders, till the defiles were shambles where men could scarcely keep their feet on the blood-washed, corpse-littered paths.

The westering sun cast long shadows across the cliff-shaded beaches when I came upon the king of the attackers. He was on a level expanse where the upward trending slope ran level for a short distance before it dipped up again at a steeper slant. Arrows had wounded him, and swords had gashed him, but the mad blaze in his eyes was undimmed, and his thundering voice still urged his gasping, weary, staggering warriors to the onset. Yet now, though the battle raged fiercely in the other defiles, he stood among a host of the dead, and only two huge warriors stood beside him, their spears clotted with blood and brains.

Kelka was at my heels as I rushed at the Vanir. The two painted warriors leaped to bar my path, but Kelka was upon them. From each side they leaped at him, their spears driving in with a hiss. Yet as a wolf avoids the stroke he writhed beyond the goring blades, and the three figures caromed together an instant; then one warrior fell away, disembowelled, and the other dropped across him, his head half severed from his body.

As I leaped toward the red-haired king, we struck simultaneously. My sword tore the helmet from his head, and at his terrible stroke, his sword and my shield shattered together. Before I could strike again, he dropped the broken hilt and grappled with me as a grizzly grapples. I let go my sword, useless at such close quarters, and closelocked, we reeled on the crest of the slope.

We were evenly matched in strength, but his might was ebbing from him with the blood of a score of wounds. Straining and gasping with the effort, we swayed, hard-braced, and I felt my pulse pound in my temples, saw the great veins swell in his. Then suddenly he gave way, and we pitched headlong, to roll down the slanting defile. In that grim strife neither dared try to draw a dagger. But as we rolled and tore at each other, I felt the iron ebbing from his mighty limbs, and by a volcanic burst of effort, heaved on top, and sunk my fingers deep in his corded throat. Sweat and blood misted my vision, my breath came in whistling gasps, but I sank my fingers deeper and deeper. His tearing hands grew aimless and groping, until with a racking gasp of effort, I tore out my dagger and drove it home again and again, until the giant lay motionless beneath me.

Then as I reeled upright, half-blinded and shaking from the desperate strife, Kelka would have hewed off the king's head, but I prevented it.

A long wavering cry went up from the invaders and they flinched for the first time. Their king had been the fire which had held them like doom to their fate all day. Now they broke suddenly and fled down the defiles, and we cut them down as they ran. We followed them down onto the beach, still slaughtering them like cattle, and as they ran to their canoes and pushed off, we waded into the water until it flowed over our shoulders, glutting our mad fury. When the last survivors, rowing madly, had passed to safety, the beach was littered with still forms, and floating bodies sprawled to the wash of the surf.

Only painted bodies lay on the beach and in the shallow water, but in the defiles, where the fighting had been fiercest, seventy of the Æsir lay dead. Of the rest of us, few there were who bore not some mark or wound.

By Ymir, that was a slaying! The sun was dipping toward the horizon when we came back from the cliffs, weary, dusty and bloody, with little breath left for singing, but with our heart glad because of the red deeds we had done. The people of Khemu did the singing for us. They swarmed out of the city in a vast shouting, cheering throng, and they laid carpets of silk, strewn with roses and gold dust, before our feet. We bore with us our wounded on litters. But first we took our dead to the beach, and broke up war-canoes to make a mighty raft, and lade it with the corpses and set it afire. And we took the red-haired king of the invaders, and laid him in his great war-canoe, with the corpses of his bravest chiefs about him to serve him in ghostland, and we gave to him the same honors we gave to our own men.

I looked eagerly for Aluna among the throng, but I did not see her. They had put up tents in the market place, and there we placed our wounded, and leeches of the Khemu came among them, and they dressed the wounds of the rest of us. Akkheba had prepared a mighty victory feast for us in his great hall, and thither we went, dust-stained and blood-stained. Even old Asgrimm grinned like a hungry wolf as he wiped the clotted blood from his knotty hands and donned the garb they had given him.

I lingered for a space among the tents where lay those too desperately wounded to walk or even be carried to the feast, hoping that Aluna would come to me. But she did not come, and I went to the great hall of the king, without which the warriors of Khemu stood at attention—three hundred of them, the more to do honor to their allies, Akkheba said.

That hall was three hundred feet in length, and half as many wide. It was floored with polished mahogany, half covered with thick rugs and leopard-skins. The walls were of carven stone, pierced by many arched, mahogany-panelled doors, and towering up to a lofty arching ceiling, and half covered with velvet tapestries. On a throne at the back of the hall, Aldheba sat, looking down at the revelry from a raised dais, with files of plumed spearmen on either side. At the great board which ran the full length of the hall, the Æsir in their battered, stained, dusty garments and corselets, many with bloody bandages, drank and roared and gorged, served by bowing slaves, both men and women.

Chiefs and nobles and warriors of the city in their burnished harnesses sat among their allies, and for each Æsir it seemed to me there were at least three or four girls, laughing, jesting, submitting to their rude caresses. Their laughter rose shrill and strident above the clamor. There was an unreality about the scene—a strained levity, a forced gaiety. But I did not see Aluna, so I turned and, passing through one of the mahogany arched doors, crossed a silken-hung chamber, and entered another. It was dimly lighted, and I almost ran into old Shakkaru. He recoiled, and seemed much put out at meeting me, for some reason or another. I noted that his hand clutched at his robe, which Akkheba had told us, all priests wore that night in our honor.

A thought occurred to me and I voiced it.

"I wish to speak to Aluna," I said. "Where is she?"

"She is at present occupied with her duties and can not see you," he said. "Come to the temple tomorrow—"

He edged away from me, and in a vague pallor underlying his swarthy complection, in a tremor behind his voice, I sensed that he was in deadly fear of me and wished to be rid of me. The suspicions of the barbarian flashed up in me. In an instant I had him by the throat, wrenching from his hand the long, wicked blade he drew from beneath his robe.

"Where is she, you jackal?" I snarled. "Tell me—or—"

He was dangling like a puppet in my grasp, his kicking heels clear of the floor, his head bent back almost to the snapping point. With the fear of death in his distended eyes, he jerked his head violently, and I eased my grasp a trifle.

"In the shrine of Ishtar," he gasped. "They sacrifice her to the goddess—spare my life—I will tell you all—the whole secret and plot—"

But I had heard enough. Whirling him on high

by girdle and knee, I dashed out his brains against a column, and leaping through an outer door, raced between rows of massive pillars, and gained the street.

A breathless silence reigned over all. No throngs were abroad that night, as one would have thought, celebrating the destruction of their enemies. The doors were shut, the windows shuttered. Hardly a light shone, and I did not even see a watchman. It was all strange and unreal; the silent, ghostly city, where the only sound was the strident, unnatural revelry rising from the great feast hall. I could see the glow of torches in the market place where our wounded lay.

I had seen old Asgrimm sitting at the head of the board, with his hands stained with dried blood, and his hacked and dusty mail showing under the silken cloak he wore; his gaunt features shadowed by the great black plumes that waved above him. All up and down the board the girls were embracing and kissing the half-drunken Æsir, lifting off their heavy helmets and easing them of their mail as they grew hot with wine.

Near the foot of the board, Kelka was tearing at a great beef-bone like a famished wolf. Some laughing girls were teasing him, coaxing him to give them his sword, until suddenly, infuriated by their sport and importunities, he dealt his foremost tormentor such a blow with the bone he was gnawing that she fell, dead or senseless, to the floor. But the high pitched laughter and wild merriment did not slacken. I likened them suddenly to vampires and skeletons, laughing over a feast of dust and ashes.

I hurried down the silent street, crossing the court and passing the houses of the priests, which seemed deserted except for slaves. Rushing into the lofty-pillared portico of the temple—I ran through the deep-lying gloom, groping in the darkness—burst into the vaguely lighted inner shrine—and halted, frozen. Lesser priests and naked women stood about the altar in positions of adoration, chanting the sacrificial song, holding golden goblets to catch the blood that ebbed down the stained grooves in the stone. And on that altar, whimpering softly as a dying doe might whimper, lay Aluna.

Shadowy was the cloud of incense smoke which gloomed the shrine; crimson as hell-fire the cloud which veiled my sight. With one inhuman yell that rang hideously to the vaulted roof, I rushed, and skulls splintered beneath my madly lashing sword. My memories of that slaughter are frenzied and chaotic. I remember frenzied screams, the whir of steel and the chop and crunch of murderous blows, the snapping of bones, spattering of blood, and the gibbering flight of figures that tore their hair and screeched to their gods as they ran—and I among them, raging in silent deadlines, like a blood-mad wolf among sheep. Some few escaped.

I remember, clear etched against a murky red background of madness, a lithe, naked woman who stood close to the altar, frozen with horror. A goblet at her lips, her eyes flaring. I caught her up with my left hand and dashed her against the marble steps with a fury that must have splintered every bone in her body. For the rest I do not well remember. There was a brief, mad whirling blast of ferocity that littered the shrine with mangled corpses. Then I stood alone among the dead, in a shrine that was a shambles, with streaks of clots and pools of blood and human fragments scattered hideously and obscenely about the dark, polished floor.

My sword trailed in a suddenly nerveless hand as I approached the altar with dragging steps. Aluna's eyelids fluttered open as I looked down at her, my hands hanging limply, my entire body sagging helplessly.

She murmured, "Hialmar!" Then her eyelids sank down, the long lashes shadowing the youthful cheek, and with a little sigh, she moved her flaxen head and lay like a child just settling to sleep. All my agonized soul cried out within me, but my lips were mute with the inarticulateness of the barbarian. I sank down upon my knees beside the altar and, groping hesitantly about her slender form with my arms, I kissed her dying lips, clumsily, falteringly, as a callow stripling might have done. That one act—that one faltering kiss—was the one touch of tenderness in the whole, hard life of Hialmar of the Æsir.

Slowly I rose, and stood above the dead girl, and as slowly and mechanically I picked up my sword. At the familiar touch of the hilt, there surged through my brain again the red fury of my race.

With a terrible cry I sprang to the marble stairs. Ishtar! They had sent her spirit shuddering up to the goddess, and close on the heels of that spirit should come the avenger! No less than the bloody goddess herself should pay for Aluna. Mine was the simple cult of the barbarian. The priests had told me that Ishtar dwelt above and the steps led to her abode. Vaguely I supposed it mounted through misty realms of stars and shadows. But up I went, to a dizzy height, until below me the shrine was but a vague play of dim lights and shadows, and darkness was all around me.

Then I came suddenly, not into a broad starry expanse of the deities, but to a grill of golden bars, and beyond them I heard a woman sobbing. But it was not Aluna's naked soul which wailed before some divine throne, for dead or alive, I knew her cry.

In mad fury I gripped the bars and they bent and buckled in my hands. Like straws I tore them aside and leaped through, my killing yell trembling in my throat. In the dim light that came from a torch set high in a niche, I saw that I was in a circular, domed chamber, whose walls and ceiling seemed to be of gold. There were velvet couches there, and silken cushions, and among these lay a naked woman, weeping. I saw the weals of a whip on her white body, and I halted, bewildered. Where was the goddess, Ishtar?

I must have spoken aloud in my barbaric Khemuri, for she lifted her head and looked at me with luminous dark eyes, swimming with tears. There was a strange beauty about her, something alien and exotic beyond my reckoning.

"I am Ishtar," she answered me, and her voice was soft as distant golden chimes, though broken now with sobbing.

"You—" I gasped, "you—Ishtar—the goddess of Khemu?"

"Yes!" she rose to her knees, wringing her white hands. "Oh, man, whoever you are—grant me one touch of mercy, if there be mercy left in the world at all! Cut my head from my body and end this long agony!"

But I drew back and lowered my sword.

"I came to slay a bloody goddess," I growled. "Not to butcher a whimpering slave girl. If you be Ishtar—who—where—in Ymir's name, what madness is this?"

"Listen, and I will tell you!" she cried, hitching toward me on her knees and catching at the skirt of my corselet. "Only listen, and then grant me the little thing I ask—the stroke of your sword!

"I am Ishtar, a daughter of a king in dim Lemuria, which the sea drank so long ago. As a child I was wed to Poseidon, god of the sea, and in the awesome mysterious bridal night, when I lay floating and unharmed on the breast of the ocean, the god gave to me the gift of life everlasting, which has become as a curse in the long centuries of my captivity.

"But I dwelt in purple Lemuria, young and beautiful, while my playmates grew old and grey about me. Then Poseidon wearied of Lemuria and of Atlantis. He rose and shook his foaming mane, and his white steeds raced over the walls and the spires and the crimson towers. But he lifted me gently on his bosom and bore me unharmed to a far land, where for many centuries I dwelt among a strange and kindly race.

"Then in an evil day I went upon a galley from distant Khitai, and in a hurricane it sank off this accursed coast. But as before I was borne gently ashore on the waves of my master, Poseidon, and the priests found me upon the beach. The people of Khemu claim descent from Lemuria, but they were a subject race, speaking a mongrel tongue. When I spoke to them in pure Lemurian, they cried out to the people that Poseidon had sent them a goddess and the people fell down and worshipped me. But the priests were devils then as now, necromancers and devil-worshippers, owning no gods save the demons of the Outer Gulfs. They pent me in this golden dome, and by cruelty they wrung my secret from me.

"For more than a thousand years I have been worshipped by the people, who were sometimes given faint glimpses of me, standing on the marble stair, half-hidden in the sacrificial smoke, or were allowed to hear my voice speaking in a strange tongue as oracle. But the priests—oh, gods of Mu, what I have suffered at their hands! Goddess to the people—slave to the priests!"

"Why do you not destroy them with your sorcery?" I demanded.

"I am no sorceress," she answered, "though you might deem me such, were I to tell you what mysteries the ages have unfolded to me. Yet there is one sorcery I might invoke—one terrible, overwhelming doom—if I might escape from this prison—if I might stand up naked in the dawn and call upon Poseidon. In the still nights I hear him roaring beyond the cliffs, but he sleeps and heeds not my cries. Yet if I might stand up in his sight and call upon him, he might hear and heed. The priests are crafty—they have shut me from his

sight and hearing—for more than a thousand years
I have not looked on the great blue monster—"

Suddenly we both started. From the city far
below us welled up a strange wild clamor.

"Treachery!" she cried. "They are murdering
your people in the streets! You destroyed the enemies they feared—now they turn on you!"

With a curse I raced down the stairs, cast one
anguished glance at the still white form on the
altar, and ran out of the temple. Down the street,
beyond the houses of the priests, rose the clanging
of steel, howls of death, yells of fury, and the thunderous war-cries of the Æsir. They were not dying
alone. The Khemuri's cries of hate and triumph
were mingled with screams of fear and pain.
Ahead of me the street seethed with battling
humanity, no more silent and deserted. From the
doors of shops, hovels and palaces alike swarmed
screeching city folk, weapons in hand, to aid their
soldiers who were locked in mad battle with the
yellow-haired aliens. Flame from a score of fires
lighted the frenzied scene like day.

As I neared the court adjoining the king's palace, along streets through which men ran howling,
an Æsir warrior staggered toward me, drift of the
storm of battle which was raging further down. He
was without armor, bent almost double, and
though an arrow stood out from his ribs, it was his
belly he was gripping with his empty hands.

"The wine was poisoned," he groaned. "We are
betrayed and doomed! We drank deep, and in our
cups the women coaxed from us our swords and
armor. Only Asgrimm and the Pict would not give
them up. Then suddenly the women slipped away,

that old vulture Akkheba left the feast hall—then
the pangs took hold on us! Ah, Ymir, it twists my
vitals like a knotted rope! Then the doors swarmed
suddenly with archers who drove their arrows
upon us—the warriors of Khemu drew their
swords and fell upon us—the priests who swarmed
the hall tore hidden blades from their robes. Hark
to the yelling in the market place where they cut
the throats of the wounded! Ymir, cold steel a man
may laugh at, but this—this—ah, Ymir!"

He sank to the pave, bent like a drawn bow,
froth drooling from his lips, his limbs jerking in
horrible convulsions. I raced into the court. On
the further side, and in the street in front of the
palace, was a mass of struggling figures.

Swarms of dark-skinned men in armor battled
with half-naked yellow-haired giants, who smote
and rent like wounded lions, though their only
weapons were broken benches, arms snatched
from dying foes, or their naked hands, and whose
lips were flecked with the froth of the agony that
knotted their entrails. I swear by Ymir, they did
not die alone; mangled corpses were trodden
under their feet, and they were like wild beasts
whose ferocity is not quenched save with the extin-
guishing of the last, least spark of life.

The great feast hall was burning. In its light I
saw, standing on the dais high above the conflict,
old Akkheba, shaking and trembling with terror at
his own treachery, with two stalwart guards on the
steps below him. The fighting scattered out over
the court, and I saw Kelka. He was drunk, but this
did not alter his deadliness. He was the center of
a struggling clump of thrusting, hacking figures,

and his long knife flashed in the firelight as it ripped through throats, and bellies, spilling blood and entrails on the marble pave.

With a low, sullen roar I charged into the thick of them, and in an instant we stood alone in a ring of corpses.

He grinned wolfishly, his teeth champing spasmodically.

"There was the devil in the wine, Hialmar! It claws at my guts like a wildcat—come, let us kill some more of them before we die. Look—the Old One makes his last stand!"

I glanced quickly where, directly in front of the blazing feast hall, Asgrimm's gaunt frame loomed among the swarming pack. I saw the flash of his sword and the dropping of men about him. An instant his black plumes waved over the horde—then they vanished and over the place he had stood rolled the dark wave.

The next instant I was leaping toward the marble stairs, with Kelka close at my heels. We smote the line of warriors on the lower steps, and burst through. They surged in behind to pull us down, but Kelka wheeled and his long blade made deadly play among them. They swarmed in on him from all sides, and there he died as he had lived, slashing and slaying in silent frenzy, neither asking quarter nor giving it.

I leaped up on the steps, and old Akkheba howled at my coming. My broken sword I had left wedged in a guardsman's breastbone. With my naked hands I charged the two guardsmen at the upper steps. They sprang to meet me, stabbing hard. I caught the driving spear of one and hurled him headlong down the stairs, to dash out his brains at the bottom. The spear of the other tore through my mail and blood gushed over the shaft. Before he could tear it free for a second thrust, I gripped his throat and tore it out with my fingers. Then wrenching forth the spear and casting it aside, I rushed at Akkheba, who screamed and sprang up, grasping the scrolled edge of the sloping stone roof behind the dais. Mad terror lent the old one strength and courage. Up the steep slope he clambered like a monkey, catching at the carved decorations with fingers and toes, and howling all the time like a beaten dog.

And I followed him. My life was ebbing out of the wound beneath my mail. It was soaked with blood, but my wild beast vitality was as yet undiminished. Up and up he climbed, shrieking, and higher and higher we rose above the city, until we swayed precariously on the level roof-ridge, five hundred feet above the howling streets. And then we were frozen, the hunted and the hunter.

A strange, haunting cry rang above the hellish tumult that raged below us, above Akkheba's frenzied howling. On the great golden dome, high above all other towers and spires, stood a naked figure, hair blown in the dawn wind, etched in the red dawn glow. It was Ishtar, waving her arms and screaming a frenzied invocation in a strange tongue. Faintly it came to us. She had escaped from the golden prison I had burst open. Now she stood on the dome, calling upon the god of her fathers, Poseidon!

But I had my own vengeance to consummate. I poised for the leap that would carry us both crashing five hundred feet to death—and under my feet the solid masonry rocked. A new frenzy rang in Akkheba's screams. With a thunderous crash the distant cliffs fell into the sea. There was a long, rumbling, cataclysmic crash, like the shattering of a world, and to my startled gaze the entire vast plain waved like a surf, gave way, and dipped southward.

Great chasms gaped in the tilting plain, and suddenly, with an indescribable rumble, a grinding thunder, and a crashing of falling walls and buckling towers, the entire city of Khemu was in motion! It was sliding in a vast, chaotic ruin down to the sea which rose, rearing, to meet it! In that sliding horror, tower crashed against tower, buckling and toppling, grinding screaming human insects to red dust, crushing them to bits with falling stones. Where I had looked out upon an ordered city, with walls and spires and roofs, all was a mad, buckled, crumpled, splintering chaos of thundering stone, where spires rocked crazily above the ruins, and came thundering down.

Still the dome rode the wrack, and the white figure upon it still screamed and gestured. Then with an awesome roar, the sea stirred and rose, and great tentacles of green foam curled mountain high and roared down over the sliding, rumbling ruins, mounting higher and higher until the entire southern side of the crushed city was hidden in swirling green waters.

For an instant the ancient roof-ridge on which we clung had risen above the ruin, holding its place. And in that instant I leaped and gripped old Akkheba. His death-shriek yowled in my ear as under my iron fingers I felt his flesh tear like rotten pulp, his thews rip from his bones, and the bones themselves splinter. The thunderings of the breaking world were in my ear, the swirling green waters at my feet, but, as the whole earth seemed to crumble and break, as the masonry dissolved beneath my feet, and the roaring green tides surged over me, drowning me in untold shimmering fathoms, my last thought was that Akkheba had died by my hand, before a wave touched him.

I sprang up with a cry, hands out thrown as if to fend off the swirling waves. I reeled, dizzy with surprise. Khemu and the eld had vanished. I stood on the oak-clad hill, and the sun hung a hand's breadth above the post-oak shinnery. Seconds only had elapsed since the woman had gestured before my eyes. Now she stood looking at me with that enigmatic smile that had less of mockery than pity.

"What is this?" I exclaimed, dazedly. "I was Hialmar—I am James Allison—the sea was the Gulf—the Great Plains ran to the shore then, and on the shore stood the accursed city of Khemu. No! I can not believe you! I can not believe my own reason. You have hypnotized me—made me dream—"

She shook her head.

"It came to pass, long, long ago, Hialmar."

"Then what of Khemu?" I exclaimed.

"Its broken ruins sleep in the deep blue waters of the Gulf, wither they washed in the long ages that passed after the breaking of the land, before the waters receded and left these long rolling steppes."

"But what of the woman Ishtar, their goddess?"

"Was she not the bride of Poseidon, who heard her cry and destroyed the evil city? On his bosom he bore her unharmed. She was deathless and eternal. She wandered through many lands, and dwelt with many people, but she had learned her lesson, and she who had been a slave of priests, became their ruler. She who had been a goddess in cruel seeming, became a goddess in her right, by virtue of her ancient wisdom.

"She was Ishtar of the Assyrians, and Ashtoreth of the Phoenicians; she was Mylitta and Belit of the Babylonians, Derketo of the Philistines. Aye, and she was Isis of Egypt, and Astarte of Carthage; and she was Freya of the Saxons, and Aphrodite of the Grecians, and Venus of the Romans. The races call her by many names, and worship her in many ways, but she is one and the same, and the fires of her altars are not quenched."

As she spoke she lifted her clear, dark luminous eyes to me; the last lurid sheen of the sunset caught the rippling glory of her hair, dusky as night, framing the strange beauty of her face, alien and exotic beyond my understanding. And a cry broke from my lips.

"You! You are Ishtar! Then it is true! And you are deathless—you are the Eternal Woman—the root and the bud of Creation—the symbol of life everlasting! And I—I was Hialmar, and knew pride and battle and far lands, and the bright glory of war—"

"As truly as you shall know them all again, oh weary one," she said softly, "when, in a little while, you shall put off that misshapen mask of broken flesh and don new raiment, bright and gleaming as the armor of Hialmar!"

Then night dipped down, and whither she went I know not, but I sat alone in the thicket-clad hill, and the night wind murmured up from the sand-drifts and the shinnery, and whispered among the dreary branches of the post-oaks.

One of the stranger settings Howard developed was the little fishing village of Faring town. From the names of the people and the climate, it might have lain on the coasts of Maine, or County Donegal, or the Yorkshire strands. Like all fishing settlements its people are familiar with death, locked in their grim theological combat with the sea.

In Faring town, however, death can be strangely transient. . . .

SEA CURSE

And some return by the failing light
  And some in the waking dream,
For she hears the heels of the dripping ghosts
  That ride the rough roofbeam.

—KIPLING

They were the brawlers and braggarts, the loud boasters and hard drinkers, of Faring town, John Kulrek and his crony Lie-lip Canool. Many a time have I, a tousled-haired lad, stolen to the tavern door to listen to their curses, their profane arguments and wild sea songs; half fearful and half in admiration of these wild rovers. Aye, all the people of Faring town gazed on them with fear and admiration, for they were not like the rest of the Faring men; they were not content to ply their trade along the coasts and among the shark-teeth shoals.

181

No yawls, no skiffs for them! They fared far, farther than any other man in the village, for they shipped on the great sailing-ships that went out on the white tides to brave the restless gray ocean and make ports in strange lands.

Ah, I mind it was swift times in the little seacoast village of Faring when John Kulrek came home, with his furtive Lie-lip at his side, swaggering down the gang-plank, in his tarry seaclothes, and the broad leather belt that held his ever-ready dagger; shouting condescending greeting to some favored acquaintance, kissing some maiden who ventured too near; then up the street, roaring some scarcely decent song of the sea. How the cringers and the idlers, the hangers-on, would swarm about the two desperate heroes, flattering and smirking, guffawing hilariously at each nasty jest. For to the tavern loafers and to some of the weaker among the straight-forward villagers, these men with their wild talk and their brutal deeds, their tales of the Seven Seas and the far countries, these men, I say, were valiant knights, nature's noblemen who dared to be men of blood and brawn.

And all feared them, so that when a man was beaten or a woman insulted, the villagers muttered—and did nothing. And so when Moll Farrell's niece was put to shame by John Kulrek, none dared even to put in words what all thought. Moll had never married, and she and the girl lived alone in a little hut down close to the beach, so close that in high tide the waves came almost to the door.

The people of the village accounted old Moll

something of a witch, and she was a grim, gaunt old dame who had little to say to anyone. But she minded her own business, and eked out a slim living by gathering clams, and picking up bits of driftwood.

The girl was a pretty, foolish little thing, vain and easily befooled, else she had never yielded to the shark-like blandishments of John Kulrek.

I mind the day was a cold winter day with a sharp breeze out of the east when the old dame came into the village street shrieking that the girl had vanished. All scattered over the beach and back among the bleak inland hills to search for her—all save John Kulrek and his cronies who sat in the tavern dicing and toping. All the while beyond the shoals, we heard the never-ceasing droning of the heaving, restless gray monster, and in the dim light of the ghostly dawn Moll Farrell's girl came home.

The tides bore her gently across the wet sands and laid her almost at her own door. Virgin-white she was, and her arms were folded across her still bosom; calm was her face, and the gray tides sighed about her slender limbs. Moll Farrell's eyes were stones, yet she stood above her dead girl and spoke no word till John Kulrek and his crony came reeling down from the tavern, their drinking-jacks still in their hands. Drunk was John Kulrek, and the people gave back for him, murder in their souls; so he came and laughed at Moll Farrell across the body of her girl.

"Zounds!" swore John Kulrek, "the wench has drowned herself, Lie-lip!"

Lie-lip laughed, with the twist of his thin mouth.

He always hated Moll Farrell, for it was she that had given him the name of Lie-lip.

Then John Kulrek lifted his drinking-jack, swaying on his uncertain legs. "A health to the wench's ghost!" he bellowed, while all stood aghast.

Then Moll Farrell spoke, and the words broke from her in a scream which sent ripples of cold up and down the spines of the throng.

"The curse of the Foul Fiend upon you, John Kulrek!" she screamed. "The curse of God rest upon your vile soul throughout eternity! May you gaze on sights that shall sear the eyes of you and scorch the soul of you! May you die a bloody death and writhe in hell's flames for a million and a million and yet a million years! I curse you by sea and by land, by earth and by air, and by the demons of the oceans and the demons of the swamplands, the fiends of the forests and the goblins of the hills! And you—" her lean finger stabbed at Lie-lip Canool and he started backward, his face paling, "you shall be the death of John Kulrek and he shall be the death of you! You shall bring John Kulrek to the doors of hell and John Kulrek shall bring you to the gallows-tree! I set the seal of death upon your brow, John Kulrek! You shall live in terror and die in horror far out upon the cold gray sea! But the sea that took the soul of innocence to her bosom shall not take you, but shall fling forth your vile carcass to the sands! Aye, John Kulrek—" and she spoke with such a terrible intensity that the drunken mockery of the man's face changed to one of swinish stupidity, "the sea roars for the victim it will not keep! There is snow upon the hills, John Kulrek, and ere it melts your corpse will lie at my feet. And I shall spit upon it and be content."

Kulrek and his crony sailed at dawn for a long voyage, and Moll went back to her hut and her clam gathering. She seemed to grow leaner and more grim than ever and her eyes smoldered with a light not sane. The days glided by and people whispered among themselves that Moll's days were numbered, for she faded to a ghost of a woman; but she went her way, refusing all aid.

That was a short, cold summer and the snow on the barren inland hills never melted; a thing very unusual, which caused much comment among the villagers. At dusk and at dawn Moll would come up on the beach, gaze up at the snow which glittered on the hills, then out to sea with a fierce intensity in her gaze.

Then the days grew shorter, the nights longer and darker, and the cold gray tides came sweeping along the bleak strands, bearing the rain and sleet of the sharp east breezes.

And upon a bleak day a trading-vessel sailed into the bay and anchored. And all the idlers and the wastrels flocked to the wharfs, for that was the ship upon which John Kulrek and Lie-lip Canool had sailed. Down the gang-plank came Lie-lip, more furtive than ever, but John Kulrek was not there.

To shouted queries, Canool shook his head. "Kulrek deserted ship at a port of Sumatra," said he. "He had a row with the skipper, lads; wanted me to desert, too, but not! I had to see you fine lads again, eh, boys?"

Almost cringing was Lie-lip Canool, and suddenly

he recoiled as Moll Farrell came through the throng. A moment they stood eyeing each other; then Moll's grim lips bent in a terrible smile.

"There's blood on your hand, Canool!" she lashed out suddenly—so suddenly that Lie-lip started and rubbed his right hand across his left sleeve.

"Stand aside, witch!" he snarled in sudden anger, striding through the crowd which gave back for him. His admirers followed him to the tavern.

Now, I mind that the next day was even colder; gray fogs came drifting out of the east and veiled the sea and the beaches. There would be no sailing that day, and so all the villagers were in their snug houses or matching tales at the tavern. So it came about that Joe, my friend, a lad of my own age, and I, were the ones who saw the first of the strange thing that happened.

Being harum-scarum lads of no wisdom, we were sitting in a small rowboat, floating at the end of the wharfs, each shivering and wishing the other would suggest leaving, there being no reason whatever for our being there, save that it was a good place to build air-castles undisturbed.

Suddenly Joe raised his hand. "Say," he said, "d'ye hear? Who can be out on the bay upon a day like this?"

"Nobody. What d'ye hear?"

"Oars. Or I'm a lubber. Listen."

There was no seeing anything in that fog, and I heard nothing. Yet Joe swore he did, and suddenly his face assumed a strange look.

"Somebody rowing out there, I tell you! The

bay is alive with oars from the sound! A score of boats at the least! Ye dolt, can ye not hear?"

Then, as I shook my head, he leaped and began to undo the painter.

"I'm off to see. Name me liar if the bay is not full of boats, all together like a close fleet. Are you with me?"

Yes, I was with him, though I heard nothing. Then out in the grayness we went, and the fog closed behind and before so that we drifted in a vague world of smoke, seeing naught and hearing naught. We were lost in no time, and I cursed Joe for leading us upon a wild goose chase that was like to end with our being swept out to sea. I thought of Moll Farrell's girl and shuddered.

How long we drifted I know not. Minutes faded into hours, hours into centuries. Still Joe swore he heard the oars, now close at hand, now far away, and for hours we followed them, steering our course toward the sound, as the noise grew or receded. This I later thought of, and could not understand.

Then, when my hands were so numb that I could no longer hold the oar, and the forerunning drowsiness of cold and exhaustion was stealing over me, bleak white stars broke through the fog which glided suddenly away, fading like a ghost of smoke, and we found ourselves afloat just outside the mouth of the bay. The waters lay smooth as a pond, all dark green and silver in the starlight, and the cold came crisper than ever. I was swinging the boat about, to put back into the bay, when Joe gave a shout, and for the first time I heard the clack of oar-locks. I glanced over my shoulder and my blood went cold.

A great beaked prow loomed above us, a weird, unfamiliar shape against the stars, and as I caught my breath, sheered sharply and swept by us, with a curious swishing I never heard any other craft make. Joe screamed and backed oars frantically, and the boat walled out of the way just in time; for though the prow had missed us, still otherwise we had died. For from the sides of the ship stood long oars, bank upon bank which swept her along. Though I had never seen such a craft, I knew her for a galley. But what was she doing upon our coasts? They said, the far-farers, that such ships were still in use among the heathens of Barbary; but it was many a long, heaving mile to Barbary, and even so she did not resemble the ships described by those who had sailed far.

We started in pursuit, and this was strange, for though the waters broke about her prow, and she seemed fairly to fly through the waves, yet she was making little speed, and it was no time before we caught up with her. Making our painter fast to a chain far back beyond the reach of the swishing oars, we hailed those on deck. But there came no answer, and at last, conquering our fears, we clambered up the chain and found ourselves upon the strangest deck man has trod for many a long, roaring century.

"This is no Barbary rover!" muttered Joe fear-somely. "Look, how old it seems! Almost ready to fall to pieces. Why, 'tis fairly rotten!"

There was no one on deck, no one at the long sweep with which the craft was steered. We stole to the hold and looked down the stair. Then and there, if ever men were on the verge of insanity, it was we. For there were rowers there, it is true; they sat upon the rowers' benches and drove the creaking oars through the gray waters. *And they that rowed were skeletons!*

Shrieking, we plunged across the deck, to fling ourselves into the sea. But at the rail I tripped upon something and fell headlong, and as I lay, I saw a thing which vanquished my fear of the horrors below for an instant. The thing upon which I had tripped was a human body, and in the dim gray light that was beginning to steal across the eastern waves I saw a dagger hilt standing up between his shoulders. Joe was at the rail, urging me to haste, and together we slid down the chain and cut the painter.

Then we stood off into the bay. Straight on kept the grim galley, and we followed, slowly, wondering. She seemed to be heading straight for the beach beside the wharfs, and as we approached, we saw the wharfs thronged with people. They had missed us, no doubt, and now they stood, there in the early dawn light, struck dumb by the apparition which had come up out of the night and the grim ocean.

Straight on swept the galley, her oars a-swish; then ere she reached the shallow water—crash!— a terrific reverberation shook the bay. Before our eyes the grim craft seemed to melt away; then she vanished, and the green waters seethed where she had ridden, but there floated no driftwood there, nor did there ever float any ashore. Aye, something floated ashore, but it was grim driftwood!

We made the landing amid a hum of excited conversation that stopped suddenly. Moll Farrell stood before her hut, limned gauntly against the ghostly dawn, her lean hand pointing seaward. And across the sighing wet sands, borne by the gray tide, something came floating; something that the waves dropped at Moll Farrell's feet. And there looked up at us, as we crowded about, a pair of unseeing eyes set in a still, white face. John Kulrek had come home.

Still and grim he lay, rocked by the tide, and as he lurched sideways, all saw the dagger hilt that stood from his back—the dagger all of us had seen a thousand times at the belt of Lie-lip Canool.

"Aye, I killed him!" came Canool's shriek, as he writhed and groveled before our gaze. "At sea on a still night in a drunken brawl I slew him and hurled him overboard! And from the far seas he has followed me—" his voice sank to a hideous whisper, "because—of—the—curse—the—sea—would—not—keep—his—body!"

And the wretch sank down, trembling, the shadow of the gallows already in his eyes.

"Aye!" Strong, deep and exultant was Moll Farrell's voice. "From the hell of lost craft Satan sent a ship of bygone ages! A ship red with gore and stained with the memory of horrid crimes! None other would bear such a vile carcass! The sea has taken vengeance and has given me mine. See now, how I spit upon the face of John Kulrek."

And with a ghastly laugh, she pitched forward, the blood starting to her lips. And the sun came up across the restless sea.

Another tale of Faring town; in which a man dies—but something else returns in his shape. . . .

OUT OF THE DEEP

Adam Falcon sailed at dawn, and Margaret Deveral, the girl who was to marry him, stood on the wharfs in the cold mist to wave a good-bye. At the dusk Margaret knelt, stony-eyed, above the still white form that the crawling tide had left crumpled on the beach.

The people of Faring town gathered about, whispering. "The fog hung heavy; mayhap she went ashore on Ghost Reef. Strange that his corpse alone should drift back to Faring harbor—and so swiftly."

And an undertone. "Alive or dead, he would come to her!"

The body lay above the tide mark, as if flung by a vagrant wave; slim, but strong and virile in life, now darkly handsome even in death. The eyes were closed, strange to say, so it appeared that he but slept. The seaman's clothes he wore had fragments of seaweed clinging to them.

"Strange," muttered old John Harper, owner of the Sea-lion Inn, and the oldest ex-seaman of Faring town. "He sank deep, for these weeds grow only at the bottom of the ocean, aye, in the coral-grown caves of the sea."

Margaret spoke no word, she but knelt, her hands pressed to her cheeks, eyes wide and staring.

"Take him in your arms, lass, and kiss him," gently urged the people of Faring, "for 'tis what he would have wished, alive."

The girl obeyed mechanically, shuddering at the coldness of the body. Then as her lips touched his, she screamed and recoiled.

"This is not Adam!" she shrieked, staring wildly about her.

The people nodded sadly to each other.

"Her brain is turned," they whispered, and then they lifted the corpse and bore it to the house wherein Adam Falcon had lived—where he had hoped to bring his bride when he returned from his voyage.

And the people brought Margaret along with them, caressing her and soothing her with gentle words. But the girl walked like one in a trance, her eyes still staring in that strange manner.

They laid the body of Adam Falcon on his bed, with death candles at the head and feet, and the salt water from his garments trickled off the bed and splashed on the floor. For it is a superstition in Faring town, as on many dim coasts, that monstrously bad luck will follow if a drowned man's clothes are removed.

And Margaret sat there in the death room and spoke to none, staring fixedly at Adam's dark calm face. And, as she sat, John Gower, a rejected suitor of hers, and a moody, dangerous man, came and, looking over her shoulder, said: "Sea death brings a curious change, if that is the Adam Falcon I knew."

Black looks were passed his way, whereat he seemed surprised; and men rose and quietly escorted him to the door.

"You hated Adam Falcon, John Gower," said Tom Leary, "and you hate Margaret because the child preferred a better man than you. Now, by Satan, you'll not be torturing the girl with your calloused talk. Get out and stay!"

Gower scowled darkly at this, but Tom Leary stood up boldly to him, and the men of Faring town back of him, so John turned his back squarely upon them and strode away. Yet to me it had seemed that what he had said had not been meant as a taunt or an insult, but simply the result of a sudden, startling thought.

And as he walked away I heard him mutter to himself, ". . . Alike, and yet strangely unlike him . . ."

Night had fallen on Faring town and the windows of the houses blinked through the darkness; through the windows of Adam Falcon's house glimmered the death candles where Margaret and others kept silent watch until dawn. And beyond the friendly warmth of the town's lights, the dusky green titan brooded along the strand, silent now as if in sleep, but ever ready to leap with hungry talons. I wandered down to the beach and, reclining on the white sand, gazed out over the slowly heaving expanse which coiled and billowed in drowsy undulations like a sleeping serpent.

The sea—the great, grey, cold-eyed woman of the ages. Her tides spoke to me as they have spoken to me since birth—in the swish of the flat waves along the sand, in the wail of the ocean-bird, in her throbbing silence. *I am very old and very wise* (brooded the sea). *I have no part of man; I slay men and even their bodies I fling back upon the cowering land. There is life in my bosom, but it is not human life* (whispered the sea); *my children hate the sons of men.*

A shriek shattered the stillness and brought me to my feet, gazing wildly about me. Above, the stars gleamed coldly, and their scintillant ghosts sparkled on the ocean's cold surface. The town lay dark and still, save for the death lights in Adam Falcon's house—and the echoes still shuddering through the pulsating silence.

I was among the first to arrive at the door of the death room and there halted aghast with the rest. Margaret Deveral lay dead upon the floor, her slender form crushed like a slim ship among shoals, and crouching over her, cradling her in his arms, was John Gower, the gleam of insanity in his wide eyes. And the death candles still flickered and leaped, but no corpse lay on Adam Falcon's bed.

"God's mercy!" gasped Tom Leary. "John Gower, ye fiend from hell, what devil's work is this?"

Gower looked up.

"I told you," he shrieked. "She knew—and I knew—'twas not Adam Falcon, that cold monster flung up by the mocking waves! 'Tis some demon inhabiting his corpse! Hark—I sought my bed and tried to sleep, but each time there came the thought of this soft girl sitting beside that cold inhuman thing you thought her lover, and at last I rose and came to the window. Margaret sat, drowsing, and the others, fools that they were slept in other parts of the house. And as I watched . . ."

He shook as a wave of shuddering passed over him.

"As I watched, Adam's eyes opened, and the corpse rose swift and stealthy from the bed where it lay. I stood without the window, frozen, helpless, and the ghastly thing stole upon the unknowing girl, with frightful eyes burning with hellish light and snaky arms outstretched. Then, she woke and screamed and then—oh Mother of God!—the dead man lapped her in his terrible arms, and she died without a sound."

Gower's voice died out into incoherent gibberings, and he rocked the dead girl gently to and fro like a mother with a child.

Tom Leary shook him. "Where is the corpse?"

"He fled into the night," said John Gower tonelessly.

Men looked at each other, bewildered.

"He lies," muttered they, deep in their beards. "He has slain Margaret himself and hidden the corpse somewhere to bear out his ghastly tale."

A sullen snarl shook the throng, and as one man they turned and looked where, on Hangman's Hill overlooking the bay, Lie-lip Canool's bleached skeleton glimmered against the stars.

They took the dead girl from Gower's arms, though he clung to her, and laid her gently on the bed between the candles meant for Adam Falcon. Still she lay, and white, and men and women whispered that she seemed more like one drowned than one crushed to death.

We bore John Gower through the village streets, he not resisting, but seeming to walk in a daze, muttering to himself. But in the square, Tom Leary halted.

"This is a strange tale Gower told us," said he, "and doubtless a lie. Still, I am not a man to be hanging another without certainty. Therefore, let us place him in the stocks for safekeeping, while we search for Adam's corpse. Time enough for hanging afterwards."

So this was done and as we turned away, I looked back upon John Gower, who sat, head bowed upon his breast, like a man who is weary unto death.

So, under the dim wharfs and in the attics of houses and among stranded hulls we searched for Adam Falcon's corpse. Back up into the hills behind the town our hunt lead us, where we broke up into groups and couples and scattered out over the barren downs.

My companion was Michael Hansen, and we had gotten so far apart that the darkness cloaked him from me, when he gave a sudden shout. I started toward him, and then the shout broke into a shriek and the shriek died off into grisly silence. Michael Hansen lay dead on the earth, and a dim form slunk away in the gloom as I stood above the corpse, my flesh crawling.

Tom Leary and the rest came on the run and gathered about, swearing that John Gower had done this deed, also.

"He has escaped, somehow, from the stocks,"

said they, and we legged it for the village at top speed.

Aye, John Gower had escaped from the stocks and from his townsmen's hate and from all the sorrows of life. He sat as we had left him, head bowed upon his breast; but One had come to him in the darkness, and, though all his bones were broken, he seemed like a drowned man.

Then stark horror fell like a thick fog on Faring town. We clustered about the stocks, struck silent, till shrieks from a house on the outskirts of the village told us that the horror had struck again, and, rushing there, we found red destruction and death. And a maniac woman who whimpered before she died that Adam Falcon's corpse had broken through the window, flaming-eyed and horrible, to rend and slay. A green slime fouled the room and fragments of seaweed clung to the window sill.

Then fear, unreasoning and shameless, took possession of the men of Faring town, and they fled to their separate houses, where they locked and bolted doors and windows and crouched behind them, weapons trembling in their hands and black terror in their souls. For what weapon can slay the dead?

And through the deathly night, horror stalked through Faring town and hunted the sons of men. Men shuddered and dared not even look forth when the crash of a door or window told the entrance of the fiend into some wretch's cottage, when shrieks and gibberings told of its grisly deeds therein.

Yet there was one man who did not shut himself

behind doors to be there slaughtered like a sheep. I was never a brave man, nor was it courage that sent me out into the ghastly night. No, it was the driving power of a Thought, a Thought which had birth in my brain as I looked on the dead face of Michael Hansen. A vague and illusive thing it was, a hovering and an almost-being—but not quite. Somewhere at the back of my skull it lurked, and I could not rest until I had proved or disproved that which I could not even formulate into a concrete theory.

So, with my brain in strange and chaotic condition, I stole through the shadows, warily. Mayhap the sea, strange and fickle even to her chosen, had whispered something to my inner mind, had betrayed her own. I know not.

But all through the dark hours I prowled along the beach, and, when in the first grey light of the early dawn, a fiendish shape came striding down to the shore, I was waiting there.

To all seeming it was Adam Flacon's corpse, animated by some horrid life, which fronted me there in the grey gloom. The eyes were open now, and they glimmered with a cold light, like the reflections of some deep sea hell. And I knew that it was not Adam Falcon who faced me.

"Sea fiend," I said in an unsteady voice, "I know not how you came by Adam Falcon's apparel. I know not whether his ship went upon the rocks, or whether he fell overboard, or whether you climbed up the strake and over the rail and dragged him from his own deck. Nor do I know by what foul ocean magic you twisted your devil's features into a likeness of his.

"But this I know. Adam Falcon sleeps in peace beneath the blue tides. You are not he. That I suspected—now I know. This horror has come upon Earth of yore—so long ago that all men have forgotten the tales; all except such as I, whom men name fool. I know, and knowing, I fear you not, and here I slay you, for though you are not human, you may be slain by a man who does not fear you—even though that man be only a youth and considered strange and foolish. You have left your demon's mark upon the land; God alone knows how many souls you have reft, how many brains you have shattered this night. The ancients said your kind could do harm only in the form of men, on land. Aye, you tricked the sons of men—were borne into their midst by kind and gentle hands— by men who knew not they carried a monster from the abysses.

"Now, you have worked your will, and the sun will soon rise. Before that time you must be far below the green waters, basking in the accursed caverns that human eye has never looked upon save in death. There lies the sea and safety; I alone bar the way."

He came upon me like a towering wave, and his arms were like green serpents about me. I knew they were crushing me; yet I felt as if I were drowning instead, and even then understood the expression that had puzzled me on Michael Hansen's face—that of a drowned man.

I was looking into the inhuman eyes of the monster, and it was as if I gazed into untold depths of oceans—depths into which I should presently tumble and drown. And I felt scales . . .

Neck, arm, and shoulder he gripped me, bending me back to break my spine, and I drove my knife into his body again—and again—and again. He roared once, the only sound I ever heard him make, and it was like the roar of the tides among the shoals. Like the pressure of a hundred fathoms of green water was the grasp upon my body and limbs, and then, as I thrust again, he gave way and crumpled to the beach.

He lay there writhing and then was still, and already he had begun to change. Merman, the ancients named his kind, knowing they were endowed with strange attributes, one of which was the ability to take the full form of a man if lifted from the ocean by the hands of men. I bent and tore the human clothing from the thing. And the first gleams of the sun fell upon a slimy and moldering mass of seaweed, from which stared two hideous dead eyes—a formless bulk that lay at the water's edge, where the first high wave would bear it back to that from which it came: the cold jade ocean deeps.

Howard had a stable of heroes: the giant Cimmerian, Conan; King Kull of ancient Atlantis; Solomon Kane, the odd Puritan who wanders the continent of Africa with arquebus and iron-bound bible, confronting the spirits of darkness. Rather oddly, one of his heroes was, in a sense, a spirit of darkness himself—under a terrible curse acquired in a French forest.

IN THE FOREST OF VILLEFÈRE

The sun had set. The great shadows came striding over the forest. In the weird twilight of a late summer day, I saw the path ahead glide on among the mighty trees and disappear. And I shuddered and glanced fearfully over my shoulder. Miles behind lay the nearest village—miles ahead the next.

I looked to left and to right as I strode on, and anon I looked behind me. And anon I stopped short, grasping my rapier, as a breaking twig betokened the going of some small beast. Or was it a beast?

But the path led on and I followed, because, forsooth, I had naught else to do.

As I went I bethought me. "My own thoughts will rout me, if I be not aware. What is there in this forest, except perhaps the creatures that roam it, deer and the like? Tush, the foolish legends of those villagers!"

And so I went and the twilight faded into dusk. Stars began to blink and the leaves of the trees murmured in the faint breeze. And then I stopped short, my sword leaping to my hand, for just ahead, around a curve of the path, someone was singing. The words I could not distinguish, but the accent was strange, almost barbaric.

I stepped behind a great tree, and the cold sweat beaded my forehead. Then the singer came in sight, a tall, thin man, vague in the twilight. I shrugged my shoulders. A *man* I did not fear. I sprang out, my point raised.

"Stand!"

He showed no surprise. "I prithee, handle thy blade with care, friend," he said.

Somewhat ashamed, I lowered my sword.

"I am new to this forest," I quoth, apologetically. "I heard talk of bandits. I crave pardon. Where lies the road to Villefère?"

"*Corbleu*, you've missed it," he answered. "You should have branched off to the right some distance back. I am going there myself. If you may abide my company, I will direct you."

I hesitated. Yet why should I hesitate?

"Why, certainly. My name is de Montour, of Normandy."

"And I am Carolus le Loup."

"No!" I started back.

He looked at me in astonishment.

"Pardon," said I; "the name is strange. Does not *loup* mean wolf?"

"My family were always great hunters," he answered. He did not offer his hand.

"You will pardon my staring," said I as we walked down the path, "but I can hardly see your face in the dusk."

I sensed that he was laughing, though he made no sound.

"It is little to look upon," he answered.

I stepped closer and then leaped away, my hair bristling.

"A mask!" I exclaimed. "Why do you wear a mask, *m'sieu?*"

"It is a vow," he explained. "In fleeing a pack of hounds I vowed that if I escaped I would wear a mask for a certain time."

"Hounds, *m'sieu?*"

"Wolves," he answered quickly; "I said wolves."

We walked in silence for a while and then my companion said, "I am surprised that you walk these woods by night. Few people come these ways even in the day."

"I am in haste to reach the border," I answered. "A treaty has been signed with the English, and the Duke of Burgundy should know of it. The people at the village sought to dissuade me. They spoke of a—wolf that was purported to roam these woods."

"Here the path branches to Villefère," said he, and I saw a narrow, crooked path that I had not seen when I passed before. It led in amid the darkness of the trees. I shuddered.

"You wish to return to the village?"

"No!" I exclaimed. "No, no! Lead on."

So narrow was the path that we walked single

file, he leading. I looked well at him. He was taller, much taller than I, and thin, wiry. He was dressed in a costume that smacked of Spain. A long rapier swung at his hip. He walked with long easy strides, noiselessly.

Then he began to talk of travel and adventure. He spoke of many lands and seas he had seen and many strange things. So we talked and went farther and farther into the forest.

I presumed that he was French, and yet he had a very strange accent, that was neither French nor Spanish nor English, nor like any language I had ever heard. Some words he slurred strangely and some he could not pronounce at all.

"This path is not often used, is it?" I asked.

"Not by many," he answered and laughed silently. I shuddered. It was very dark and the leaves whispered together among the branches.

"A fiend haunts this forest," I said.

"So the peasants say," he answered, "but I have roamed it oft and have never seen his face."

Then he began to speak of strange creatures of darkness, and the moon rose and shadows glided among the trees. He looked up at the moon.

"Haste!" said he. "We must reach our destination before the moon reaches her zenith."

We hurried along the trail.

"They say," I said, "that a werewolf haunts these woodlands."

"It might be," said he, and we argued much upon the subject.

"The old women say," said he, "that if a werewolf is slain while a wolf, then he is slain, but if he is slain as a man, then his half-soul will haunt his slayer forever. But haste thee, the moon nears her zenith."

We came into a small moonlit glade and the stranger stopped.

"Let us pause a while," said he.

"Nay, let us be gone," I urged; "I like not this place."

He laughed without sound. "Why," said he, "this is a fair glade. As good as a banquet hall it is, and many times have I feasted here. Ha, ha, ha! Look ye, I will show you a dance." And he began bounding here and there, anon flinging back his head and laughing silently. Thought I, the man is mad.

As he danced his weird dance I looked about me. *The trail went not on but stopped in the glade.*

"Come," said I, "we must on. Do you not smell the rank, hairy scent that hovers about the glade? Wolves den here. Perhaps they are about us and are gliding upon us even now."

He dropped upon all fours, bounded higher than my head, and came toward me with a strange slinking motion.

"That dance is called the Dance of the Wolf," said he, and my hair bristled.

"Keep off!" I stepped back, and with a screech that set the echoes shuddering he leaped for me, and though a sword hung at his belt he did not draw it. My rapier was half out when he grasped my arm and flung me headlong. I dragged him with me and we struck the ground together. Wrenching a hand free I jerked off the mask. A shriek of horror broke from my lips. Beast eyes glittered beneath that mask, white fangs flashed in the moonlight. *The face was that of a wolf.*

In an instant those fangs were at my throat. Taloned hands tore the sword from my grasp. I beat at that horrible face with my clenched fists, but his jaws were fastened on my shoulder, his talons tore at my throat. Then I was on my back. The world was fading. Blindly I struck out. My hand dropped, then closed automatically about the hilt of my dagger, which I had been unable to get at. I drew and stabbed. A terrible, half-bestial bellowing screech. Then I reeled to my feet, free. At my feet lay the werewolf.

I stooped, raised the dagger, then paused, looked up. The moon hovered close to her zenith. *If I slew the thing as a man its frightful spirit would haunt me forever.* I sat down waiting. The *thing* watched me with flaming wolf eyes. The long wiry limbs seemed to shrink, to crook; hair seemed to grow upon them. Fearing madness, I snatched up the *thing*'s own sword and hacked it to pieces. Then I flung the sword away and fled.

Howard returned to Africa time and time again; he regarded it—as was common in his day—as the wellspring of incorrigible savagery. That is not to say he despised it; to Howard, the savage and the strong were one. Here his werewolf hero shows a spirit more indomitable than the one which inhabits and dominates his mind. Most of Howard's protagonists were wolfsheads in the old sense of the term: outlaws, outcasts, exiles from home and family and the safe course of daily life. De Montour is a wolfshead in truth. . . .

WOLFSHEAD

Fear? your pardon, *Messieurs*, but the meaning of fear you do not know. No, I hold to my statement. You are soldiers, adventurers. You have known the charges of regiments of dragoons, the frenzy of windlashed seas. But fear, real hair-raising, horror-crawling fear, you have not known. I myself have known such fear; but until the legions of darkness swirl from hell's gate and the world flames to ruin, will never such fear again be known to men.

Hark, I will tell you the tale; for it was many years ago and half across the world, and none of you will ever see the man of whom I tell you, or seeing, know.

Return, then, with me across the years to a day when I, a reckless young cavalier, stepped from the small boat that had landed me from the ship floating in the harbor, cursed the mud that littered the crude wharf, and strode up the landing toward the castle, in answer to the invitation of an old friend, Dom Vincente da Lusto.

Dom Vincente was a strange, farsighted man—a strong man, one who saw visions beyond the ken of his time. In his veins, perhaps, ran the blood of those old Phoenicians who, the priests tell us, ruled the seas and built cities in far lands, in the dim ages. His plan of fortune was strange and yet successful; few men would have thought of it; fewer could have succeeded. For his estate was upon the western coast of that dark, mystic continent, that baffler of explorers—Africa.

There by a small bay had he cleared away the sullen jungle, built his castle and his storehouses, and with ruthless hand had he wrested the riches of the land. Four ships he had: three smaller craft and one great galleon. These plied between his domains and the cities of Spain, Portugal, France, and even England, laden with rare woods, ivory, slaves; the thousand strange riches that Dom Vincente had gained by trade and by conquest.

Aye, a wild venture, a wilder commerce. And yet might he have shaped an empire from the dark land, had it not been for the rat-faced Carlos, his nephew—but I run ahead of my tale.

Look, *Messieurs*, I draw a map on the table, thus, with finger dipped in wine. Here lay the small, shallow harbor, and here the wide wharves. A landing ran thus, up the slight slope with hutlike warehouses on each side, and here it stopped at a wide, shallow moat. Over it went a narrow draw-bridge and then one was confronted with a high palisade of logs set in the ground. This extended entirely around the castle. The castle itself was built on the model of another, earlier age; being more for strength than beauty. Built of stone brought from a great distance; years of labor and a thousand Negroes toiling beneath the lash had reared its walls, and now, completed, it offered an almost impregnable appearance. Such was the intention of its builders, for Barbary pirates ranged the coasts, and the horror of a native uprising lurked ever near.

A space of about a half-mile on every side of the castle was kept cleared away and roads had been built through the marshy land. All this had required an immense amount of labor, but man-power was plentiful. A present to a chief, and he furnished all that was needed. And Portuguese know how to make men work!

Less than three hundred yards to the east of the castle ran a wide, shallow river, which emptied into the harbor. The name has entirely slipt my mind. It was a heathenish title and I could never lay my tongue to it.

I found that I was not the only friend invited to the castle. It seems that once a year or some such matter, Dom Vincente brought a host of jolly companions to his lonely estate and made merry for some weeks, to make up for the work and solitude of the rest of the year.

In fact, it was nearly night, and a great banquet was in progress when I entered. I was acclaimed with great delight, greeted boisterously by friends and introduced to such strangers as were there.

Entirely too weary to take much part in the revelry, I ate, drank quietly, listened to the toasts and songs, and studied the feasters.

Dom Vincente, of course, I knew, as I had been intimate with him for years; also his pretty niece, Ysabel, who was one reason I had accepted his invitation to come to that stinking wilderness. Her second cousin, Carlos, I knew and disliked—a sly, mincing fellow with a face like a mink's. Then there was my old friend, Luigi Verenza, an Italian; and his flirt of a sister, Marcita, making eyes at the men as usual. Then there was a short, stocky German who called himself Baron von Schiller; and Jean Desmarte, an out-at-the-elbows nobleman of Gascony; and Don Florenzo de Seville, a lean, dark, silent man, who called himself a Spaniard and wore a rapier nearly as long as himself.

There were others, men and women, but it was long ago and all their names and faces I do not remember.

But there was one man whose face somehow drew my gaze as an alchemist's magnet draws steel. He was a leanly built man of slightly more than medium height, dressed plainly, almost austerely, and he wore a sword almost as long as the Spaniard's.

But it was neither his clothes nor his sword which attracted my attention. It was his face. A refined, high-bred face, it was furrowed deep with lines that gave it a weary, haggard expression. Tiny scars flecked jaw and forehead as if torn by savage claws; I could have sworn the narrow gray eyes had a fleeting, haunted look in their expression at times.

I leaned over to that flirt, Marcita, and asked the name of the man, as it had slipt my mind that we had been introduced.

"De Montour, from Normandy," she answered. "A strange man, I don't think I like him."

"Then he resists your snares, my little enchantress?" I murmured, long friendship making me as immune from her anger as from her wiles. But she chose not to be angry and answered coyly, glancing from under demurely lowered lashes.

I watched de Montour much, feeling somehow a strange fascination. He ate lightly, drank much, seldom spoke, and then only to answer questions.

Presently, toasts making the rounds, I noticed his companions urging him to rise and give a health. At first he refused, then rose, upon their repeated urgings, and stood silent for a moment, goblet raised. He seemed to dominate, to overawe the group of revelers. Then with a mocking, savage laugh, he lifted the goblet above his head.

"To Solomon," he exclaimed, "who bound all devils! And thrice cursed be he for that some escaped!"

A toast and a curse in one! It was drunk silently, and with many sidelong, doubting glances.

That night I retired early, weary of the long sea voyage and my head spinning from the strength of the wine, of which Dom Vincente kept such great stores.

My room was near the top of the castle and looked out toward the forests of the south and the river. The room was furnished in crude, barbaric splendor, as was all the rest of the castle.

Going to the window, I gazed out at the arquebusier pacing the castle grounds just inside the palisade; at the cleared space lying unsightly barren in the moonlight; at the forest beyond; at the silent river.

From the native quarters close to the river bank came the weird twanging of some rude lute, sounding a barbaric melody.

In the dark shadows of the forest some uncanny nightbird lifted a mocking voice. A thousand minor notes sounded—birds, and beasts, and the devil knows what else! Some great jungle cat began a hair-lifting yowling. I shrugged my shoulders and turned from the windows. Surely devils lurked in those somber depths.

There came a knock at my door and I opened it, to admit de Montour.

He strode to the window and gazed at the moon, which rode resplendent and glorious.

"The moon is almost full, is it not, *Monsieur*?" he remarked, turning to me. I nodded, and I could have sworn that he shuddered.

"Your pardon, *Monsieur*. I will not annoy you further." He turned to go, but at the door turned and retraced his steps.

"*Monsieur*," he almost whispered, with a fierce intensity, "whatever you do, be sure you bar and bolt your door tonight!"

Then he was gone, leaving me to stare after him bewilderedly.

I dozed off to sleep, the distant shouts of the revelers in my ears, and though I was weary, or perhaps because of it, I slept lightly. While I never really awoke until morning, sounds and noises seemed to drift to me through my veil of slumber, and once it seemed that something was prying and shoving against the bolted door.

As is to be supposed, most of the guests were in a beastly humor the following day and remained in their rooms most of the morning or else straggled down late. Besides Dom Vincente there were really only three of the masculine members sober: de Montour; the Spaniard, de Seville (as he called himself); and myself. The Spaniard never touched wine, and though de Montour consumed incredible quantities of it, it never affected him in any way.

The ladies greeted us most graciously.

"S'truth, *Signor*," remarked that minx Marcita, giving me her hand with a gracious air that was like to make me snicker, "I am glad to see there are gentlemen among us who care more for our company than for the wine cup; for most of them are most surprisingly befuddled this morning."

Then with a most outrageous turning of her wondrous eyes, "Methinks someone was too drunk to be discreet last night—or not drunk enough. For unless my poor senses deceive me much, someone came fumbling at my door late in the night."

"Ha!" I exclaimed in quick anger, "some—!"

"No. Hush." She glanced about as if to see that we were alone, then: "Is it not strange that Signor de Montour, before he retired last night, instructed me to fasten my door firmly?"

"Strange," I murmured, but did not tell her that he had told me the same thing.

"And is it not strange, Pierre, that though Signor de Montour left the banquet hall even before you did, yet he has the appearance of one who has been up all night?"

I shrugged. A woman's fancies are often strange.

"Tonight," she said roguishly, "I will leave my door unbolted and see whom I catch."

"You will do no such thing."

She showed her little teeth in a contemptuous smile and displayed a small, wicked dagger.

"Listen, imp. De Montour gave me the same warning he did you. Whatever he knew, whoever prowled the halls last night, the object was more apt murder than amorous adventure. Keep you your doors bolted. The lady Ysabel shares your room, does she not?"

"Not she. And I send my woman to the slave quarters at night," she murmured, gazing mischievously at me from beneath drooping eyelids.

"One would think you a girl of no character from your talk," I told her, with the frankness of youth and of long friendship. "Walk with care, young lady, else I tell your brother to spank you."

And I walked away to pay my respects to Ysabel. The Portuguese girl was the very opposite of Marcita, being a shy, modest young thing, not so beautiful as the Italian, but exquisitely pretty in an appealing, almost childish air. I once had thoughts—Hi ho! To be young and foolish!

Your pardon, *Messieurs*. An old man's mind wanders. It was of de Montour that I meant to tell you—de Montour and Dom Vincente's mink-faced cousin.

A band of armed natives were thronged about the gates, kept at a distance by the Portuguese soldiers. Among them were some score of young men and women all naked, chained neck to neck. Slaves they were, captured by some warlike tribe and brought for sale. Dom Vincente looked them over personally.

Followed a long haggling and bartering, of which I quickly wearied and turned away, wondering that a man of Dom Vincente's rank could so demean himself as to stoop to trade.

But I strolled back when one of the natives of the village nearby came up and interrupted the sale with a long harangue to Dom Vincente.

While they talked de Montour came up, and presently Dom Vincente turned to us and said, "One of the woodcutters of the village was torn to pieces by a leopard or some such beast last night. A strong young man and unmarried."

"A leopard? Did they see it?" suddenly asked de Montour, and when Dom Vincente said no, that it came and went in the night, de Montour lifted a trembling hand and drew it across his forehead, as if to brush away cold sweat.

"Look you, Pierre," quoth Dom Vincente, "I have here a slave who, wonder of wonders, desires to be your man. Though the devil only knows why."

He led up a slim young Jakri, a mere youth, whose main asset seemed a merry grin.

"He is yours," said Dom Vincente. "He is goodly trained and will make a fine servant. And look ye, a slave is of an advantage over a servant, for all he requires is food and a loin-cloth or so with a touch of the whip to keep him in his place."

It was not long before I learned why Gola wished to be "my man," choosing me among all the rest. It was because of my hair. Like many dandies of that day, I wore it long and curled, the strands falling to my shoulders. As it happened, I was the only man of the party who so wore my hair, and Gola would sit and gaze at it in silent admiration for hours at a time, or until, growing nervous under his unblinking scrutiny, I would boot him forth.

It was that night that a brooding animosity, hardly apparent, between Baron von Schiller and Jean Desmarte broke out into a flame.

As usual, a woman was the cause. Marcita carried on a most outrageous flirtation with both of them.

That was not wise. Desmarte was a wild young fool. Von Schiller was a lustful beast. But when, *Messieurs*, did woman ever use wisdom?

Their hate flamed to a murderous fury when the German sought to kiss Marcita.

Swords were clashing in an instant. But before Dom Vincente could thunder a command to halt, Luigi was between the combatants and had beaten their swords down, hurling them back viciously.

"*Signori*," said he softly, but with a fierce intensity, "is it the part of high-bred *signori* to fight over my sister? Ha, by the toe-nails of Satan, for the toss of a coin I would call you both out! You, Marcita, go to your chamber, instantly, nor leave until I give you permission."

And she went, for, independent though she was, none cared to face the slim, effeminate-appearing youth when a tigerish snarl curled his lips, a murderous gleam lightened his dark eyes.

Apologies were made, but from the glances the two rivals threw at each other, we knew that the quarrel was not forgotten and would blaze forth again at the slightest pretext.

Late that night I woke suddenly with a strange, eery feeling of horror. Why, I could not say. I rose, saw that the door was firmly bolted, and seeing Gola asleep on the floor, kicked him awake irritably.

And just as he got up, hastily, rubbing himself, the silence was broken by a wild scream, a scream that rang through the castle and brought a startled shout from the arquebusier pacing the palisade; a scream from the mouth of a girl, frenzied with terror.

Gola squawked and dived behind the divan. I jerked the door open and raced down the dark corridor. Dashing down a winding stair, I caromed into someone at the bottom and we tumbled headlong.

He gasped something and I recognized the voice of Jean Desmarte. I hauled him to his feet, and raced along, he followed; the screams had ceased, but the whole castle was in an uproar, voices shouting, the clank of weapons, lights flashing up, Dom Vincente's voice shouting for the soldiers, the noise of armed men rushing through the rooms and falling over each other. With all the confusion, Desmarte, the Spaniard, and I reached

Marcita's room just as Luigi darted inside and snatched his sister into his arms.

Others rushed in, carrying lights and weapons, shouting, demanding to know what was occurring.

The girl lay quietly in her brother's arms, her dark hair loose and rippling over her shoulders, her dainty night-garments torn to shreds and exposing her lovely body. Long scratches showed upon her arms, breasts and shoulders.

Presently she opened her eyes, shuddered, then shrieked wildly and clung frantically to Luigi, begging him not to let something take her.

"The door!" she whimpered. "I left it unbarred. And *something* crept into my room through the darkness. I struck at it with my dagger and it hurled me to the floor, tearing, tearing at me. Then I fainted."

"Where is von Schiller?" asked the Spaniard, a fierce light in his dark eyes. Every man glanced at his neighbor. All the guests were there except the German. I noted de Montour, gazing at the terrified girl, his face more haggard than usual. And I thought it strange that he wore no weapon.

"Aye, von Schiller!" exclaimed Desmarte fiercely. And half of us followed Dom Vincente out into the corridor. We began a vengeful search through the castle, and in a small, dark hallway we found von Schiller. On his face he lay, in a crimson, ever widening stain.

"This is the work of some native!" exclaimed Desmarte, face aghast.

"Nonsense," bellowed Dom Vincente. "No native from the outside could pass the soldiers. All slaves, von Schiller's among them, were barred and bolted in the slave quarters, except Gola, who sleeps in Pierre's room, and Ysabel's woman."

"But who else could have done this deed?" exclaimed Desmarte in a fury.

"You!" I said abruptly; "else why ran you so swiftly away from the room of Marcita?"

"Curse you, you lie!" he shouted, and his swift-drawn sword leaped for my breast; but quick as he was, the Spaniard was quicker. Desmarte's rapier clattered against the wall and Desmarte stood like a statue, the Spaniard's motionless point just touching his throat.

"Bind him," said the Spaniard without passion.

"Put down your blade, Don Florenzo," commanded Dom Vincente, striding forward and dominating the scene. "Signor Desmarte, you are one of my best friends, but I am the only law here and duty must be done. Give your word that you will not seek to escape."

"I give it," replied the Gascon calmly. "I acted hastily. I apologize. I was not intentionally running away, but the halls and corridors of this cursed castle confuse me."

Of us all, probably but one man believed him.

"*Messieurs!*" De Montour stepped forward. "This youth is not guilty. Turn the German over."

Two soldiers did as he asked. De Montour shuddered, pointing. The rest of us glanced once, then recoiled in horror.

"Could man have done that thing?"

"With a dagger—" began someone.

"No dagger makes wounds like that," said the Spaniard. "The German was torn to pieces by the talons of some frightful beast."

We glanced about us, half expecting some hideous monster to leap upon us from the shadows.

We searched that castle; every foot, every inch of it. And we found no trace of any beast.

Dawn was breaking when I returned to my room, to find that Gola had barred himself in; and it took me nearly a half-hour to convince him to let me in.

Having smacked him soundly and berated him for his cowardice, I told him what had taken place, as he could understand French and could speak in a weird mixture which he proudly called French.

His mouth gaped and only the whites of his eyes showed as the tale reached its climax.

"Ju-ju!" he whispered fearsomely. "Fetish man!"

Suddenly an idea came to me. I had heard vague tales, little more than hints of legends, of the devilish leopard cult that existed on the West Coast. No white man had ever seen one of its votaries, but Dom Vincente had told us tales of beast-men, disguised in skins of leopards, who stole through the midnight jungle and slew and devoured. A ghastly thrill traveled up and down my spine and in an instant I had Gola in a grasp which made him yell.

"Was that a leopard-man?" I hissed, shaking him viciously.

"Massa, massa!" he gasped. "Me good boy! Juju man get! More besser no tell!"

"You'll tell me!" I gritted, renewed my endeavors, until, his hands waving feeble protests, he promised to tell me what he knew.

"No leopard-man!" he whispered, and his eyes grew big with supernatural fear. "Moon, he full, woodcutter find, him heap clawed. Find 'nother woodcutter. Big Massa (Dom Vincente) say, 'leopard'. No leopard. But leopardman, he come to kill. *Something kill leopard-man!* Heap claw! Hai, hai! Moon full again. Something come in lonely hut; claw um woman, claw um pick'nin. Man find um claw up. Big Massa say 'leopard'. Full moon again, and woodcutter find, heap clawed. Now come in castle. No leopard. *But always footmarks of a man!"*

I gave a startled, incredulous exclamation.

It was true, Gola averred. Always the footprints of a man led away from the scene of the murder. Then why did the natives not tell the Big Massa that he might hunt down the fiend? Here Gola assumed a crafty expression and whispered in my ear, *"The footprints were of a man who wore shoes!"*

Even assuming that Gola was lying, I felt a thrill of unexplainable horror. Who, then, did the natives believe was doing these frightful murders?

And he answered: Dom Vincente!

By this time, *Messieurs*, my mind was in a whirl. What was the meaning of all this? Who slew the German and sought to ravish Marcita? And as I reviewed the crime, it appeared to me that murder rather than rape was the object of the attack.

Why did de Montour warn us, and then appear to have knowledge of the crime, telling us that Desmarte was innocent and then proving it?

It was all beyond me.

The tale of the slaughter got among the natives, in spite of all we could do, and they appeared restless and nervous, and thrice that day Dom

Vincente had a black lashed for insolence. A brooding atmosphere pervaded the castle.

I considered going to Dom Vincente with Gola's tale, but decided to wait a while.

The women kept their chambers that day, the men were restless and moody. Dom Vincente announced that the sentries would be doubled and some would patrol the corridors of the castle itself. I found myself musing cynically that if Gola's suspicions were true, sentries would be of little good.

I am not, *Messieurs*, a man to brook such a situation with patience. And I was young then. So as we drank before retiring, I flung my goblet on the table and angrily announced that in spite of man, beast or devil, I slept that night with doors flung wide. And I tramped angrily to my chamber.

Again, as on the first night, de Montour came. And his face was as a man who has looked into the gaping gates of hell.

"I have come," he said, "to ask you—nay, *Monsieur*, to implore you—to reconsider your rash determination."

I shook my head impatiently.

"You are resolved? Yes? Then I ask you to do this for me, that after I enter my chamber, you will bolt my doors from the outside."

I did as he asked, and then made my way back to my chamber, my mind in a maze of wonderment. I had sent Gola to the slave quarters, and I laid rapier and dagger close at hand. Nor did I go to bed, but crouched in a great chair, in the darkness. Then I had much ado to keep from sleeping. To keep myself awake, I fell to musing on the strange words of de Montour. He seemed to be laboring under great excitement; his eyes hinted of ghastly mysteries known to him alone. And yet his face was not that of a wicked man.

Suddenly the notion took me to go to his chamber and talk with him.

Walking those dark passages was a shuddersome task, but eventually I stood before de Montour's door. I called softly. Silence. I reached out a hand and felt splintered fragments of wood. Hastily I struck flint and steel which I carried, and the flaming tinder showed the great oaken door sagging on its mighty hinges; showed a door smashed and splintered *from the inside*. And the chamber of de Montour was unoccupied.

Some instinct prompted me to hurry back to my room, swiftly but silently, shoeless feet treading softly. And as I neared the door, I was aware of something in the darkness before me. Something which crept in from a side corridor and glided stealthily along.

In a wild panic of fear I leaped, striking wildly and aimlessly in the darkness. My clenched fist encountered a human head, and something went down with a crash. Again I struck a light; a man lay senseless on the floor and he was de Montour.

I thrust a candle into a niche in the wall, and just then de Montour's eyes opened and he rose uncertainly.

"You!" I exclaimed, hardly knowing what I said. "You, of all men!"

He merely nodded.

"You killed von Schiller?"

"Yes."

I recoiled with a gasp of horror.

"Listen." He raised his hand. "Take your rapier and run me through. No man will touch you."

"No," I exclaimed. "I can not."

"Then, quick," he said hurriedly, "get into your chamber and bolt the door. Haste! It will return!"

"What will return?" I asked, with a thrill of horror. "If it will harm me, it will harm you. Come into the chamber with me."

"No, no!" he fairly shrieked, springing back from my out-stretched arm. "Haste, haste! It left me for an instant, but it will return." Then in a low-pitched voice of indescribable horror: "It is returning. *It is here now!*"

And I felt a something, a formless, shapeless presence near. A thing of frightfulness.

De Montour was standing, legs braced, arms thrown back, fists clenched. The muscles bulged beneath his skin, his eyes widened and narrowed, the veins stood out upon his forehead as if in great physical effort. As I looked, to my horror, out of nothing, a shapeless, nameless *something* took vague form! Like a shadow it moved upon de Montour.

It was hovering about him! Good God, it was merging, becoming one with the man!

De Montour swayed; a great gasp escaped him. The dim thing vanished. De Montour wavered. Then he turned toward me, and may God grant that I never look on a face like that again!

It was a hideous, a bestial face. The eyes gleamed with a frightful ferocity; the snarling lips were drawn back from gleaming teeth, which to my startled gaze appeared more like bestial fangs than human teeth.

Silently the *thing* (I can not call it a human) slunk toward me. Gasping with horror I sprang back and through the door, just as the *thing* launched itself through the air, with a sinuous motion which even then made me think of a leaping wolf, I slammed the door, holding it against the frightful *thing* which hurled itself again and again against it.

Finally it desisted and I heard it slink stealthily off down the corridor. Faint and exhausted I sat down, waiting, listening. Through the open window wafted the breeze, bearing all the scents of Africa, the spicy and the foul. From the native village came the sound of a native drum. Other drums answered farther up the river and back in the bush. Then from somewhere in the jungle, horridly incongruous, sounded the long, high-pitched call of a timber wolf. My soul revolted.

Dawn brought a tale of terrified villagers, of a Negro woman torn by some fiend of the night, barely escaping. And to de Montour I went.

On the way I met Dom Vincente. He was perplexed and angry.

"Some hellish thing is at work in this castle," he said. "Last night, though I have said naught of it to anyone, something leaped upon the back of one of the arquebusiers, tore the leather jerkin from his shoulders and pursued him to the barbican. More, someone locked de Montour into his room last night, and he was forced to smash the door to get out."

He strode on, muttering to himself, and I proceeded down the stairs, more puzzled than ever.

De Montour sat upon a stool, gazing out the

window. An indescribable air of weariness was about him.

His long hair was uncombed and tousled, his garments were tattered. With a shudder I saw faint crimson stains upon his hands, and noted that the nails were torn and broken.

He looked up as I came in, and waved me to a seat. His face was worn and haggard, but was that of a man.

After a moment's silence, he spoke.

"I will tell you my strange tale. Never before has it passed my lips, and why I tell you, knowing that you will not believe me, I can not say."

And then I listened to what was surely the wildest, the most fantastic, the weirdest tale ever heard by man.

"Years ago," said de Montour, "I was upon a military mission in northern France. Alone, I was forced to pass through the fiend-haunted woodlands of Villefère. In those frightful forests I was beset by an inhuman, a ghastly *thing*—a werewolf. Beneath a midnight moon we fought, and I slew it. Now this is the truth: that if a werewolf is slain in the half-form of a man, its ghost will haunt its slayer through eternity. But if it is slain as a wolf, hell gapes to receive it. The true werewolf is not (as many think) a man who may take the form of a wolf, *but a wolf who takes the form of a man!*

"Now listen, my friend, and I will tell you of the wisdom, the hellish knowledge that is mine, gained through many a frightful deed, imparted to me amid the ghastly shadows of midnight forests where fiends and half-beasts roamed.

"In the beginning, the world was strange,

misshapen. Grotesque beasts wandered through its jungles. Driven from another world, ancient demons and fiends came in great numbers and settled upon this newer, younger world. Long the forces of good and evil warred.

"A strange beast, known as man, wandered among the other beasts, and since good or bad must have a concrete form ere either accomplishes its desire, the spirits of good entered man. The fiends entered other beasts, reptiles and birds; and long and fiercely waged the age-old battle. But man conquered. The great dragons and serpents were slain and with them the demons. Finally, Solomon, wise beyond the ken of man, made great war upon them, and by virtue of his wisdom, slew, seized and bound. But there were some which were the fiercest, the boldest, and though Solomon drove them out he could not conquer them. Those had taken the form of wolves. As the ages passed, wolf and demon became merged. No longer could the fiend leave the body of the wolf at will. In many instances, the savagery of the wolf overcame the subtlety of the demon and enslaved him, so the wolf became again only a beast, a fierce, cunning beast, but merely a beast. But of the werewolves, there are many, even yet.

"And during the time of the full moon, the wolf may take the form, or the half-form, of a man. When the moon hovers at her zenith, however, the wolf-spirit again takes ascendency and the werewolf becomes a true wolf once more. But if it is slain in the form of a man, then the spirit is free to haunt its slayer through the ages.

"Harken now, I had thought to have slain the

thing after it had changed to its true shape. But I slew it an instant too soon. The moon, though it approached the zenith, had not yet reached it, nor had the *thing* taken on fully the wolf-form.

"Of this I knew nothing and went my way. But when the next time approached for the full moon, I began to be aware of a strange, malicious influence. An atmosphere of horror hovered in the air and I was aware of inexplicable, uncanny impulses.

"One night in a small village in the center of a great forest, the influence came upon me with full power. It was night, and the moon, nearly full, was rising over the forest. And between the moon and me, I saw, floating in the upper air, ghostly and barely discernible, *the outline of a wolf's head*!

"I remember little of what happened thereafter. I remember, dimly, clambering into the silent street, remember struggling, resisting briefly, vainly, and the rest is a crimson maze, until I came to myself the next morning and found my garments and hands caked and stained crimson; and heard the horrified chattering of the villagers, telling of a pair of clandestine lovers, slaughtered in a ghastly manner, scarcely outside the village, torn to pieces as if by wolves.

"From that village I fled aghast, but I fled not alone. In the day I could not feel the drive of my fearful captor, but when night fell and the moon rose, I ranged the silent forest, a frightful thing, a slayer of humans, a fiend in a man's body.

"God, the battles I have fought! But always it overcame me and drove me ravening after some new victim. But after the moon had passed its fullness, the *thing's* power over me ceased suddenly.

Nor did it return until three nights before the moon was full again.

"Since then I have roamed the world—fleeing, fleeing, seeking to escape. Always the *thing* follows, taking possession of my body when the moon is full. Gods, the frightful deeds I have done!

"I would have slain myself long ago but I dare not. For the soul of a suicide is accurst, and my soul would be forever hunted through the flames of hell. And harken, most frightful of all, my slain body would forever roam the earth, moved and inhabited by the soul of the werewolf! Can any thought be more ghastly?

"And I seem immune to the weapons of man. Swords have pierced me, daggers have hacked me. I am covered with scars. Yet never have they struck me down. In Germany they bound and led me to the block. There would I have willingly placed my head, but the *thing* came upon me, and breaking my bonds, I slew and fled. Up and down the world I have wandered, leaving horror and slaughter in my trail. Chains, cells can not hold me. The *thing* is fastened to me through all eternity.

"In desperation I accepted Dom Vincente's invitation, for look you, none knows of my frightful double life, since no one could recognize me in the clutch of the demon; and few, seeing me, live to tell of it.

"My hands are red, my soul doomed to everlasting flames, my mind is torn with remorse for my crimes. And yet I can do nothing to help myself. Surely, Pierre, no man ever knew the hell that I have known.

"Yes, I slew von Schiller, and I sought to destroy the girl, Marcita. Why I did not, I can not say, for I have slain both women and men.

"Now, if you will, take your sword and slay me, and with my last breath I will give you the good God's blessing. No?

"You know now my tale and you see before you a man, fiend-haunted for all eternity."

My mind was spinning with wonderment as I left the room of de Montour. What to do, I knew not. It seemed likely that he would murder us all, and yet I could not bring myself to tell Dom Vincente all. From the bottom of my soul I pitied de Montour.

So I kept my peace, and in the days that followed I made occasion to seek him out and converse with him. A real friendship sprang up between us.

About this time that black devil, Gola, began to wear an air of suppressed excitement, as if he knew something he wished desperately to tell, but would not or else dared not.

So the days passed in feasting, drinking and hunting, until one night de Montour came to my chamber and pointed silently at the moon which was just rising.

"Look ye," he said, "I have a plan. I will give it out that I am going into the jungle for hunting and will go forth, apparently for several days. But at night I will return to the castle, and you must lock me into the dungeon which is used as a storeroom."

This we did, and I managed to slip down twice a day and carry food and drink to my friend. He insisted on remaining in the dungeon even in the day, for though the fiend had never exerted its influence over him in the daytime, and he believed it powerless then, yet he would take no chances.

It was during this time that I began to notice that Dom Vincente's mink-faced cousin, Carlos, was forcing his attentions upon Ysabel, who was his second cousin, and who seemed to resent those attentions.

Myself, I would have challenged him for a duel for the toss of a coin, for I despised him, but it was really none of my affair. However, it seemed that Ysabel feared him.

My friend Luigi, by the way, had become enamored of the dainty Portuguese girl, and was making swift love to her daily.

And de Montour sat in his cell and reviewed his ghastly deeds until he battered the bars with his bare hands.

And Don Florenzo wandered about the castle grounds like a dour Mephistopheles.

And the other guests rode and quarreled and drank.

And Gola slithered about, eyeing me as if always on the point of imparting momentous information. What wonder if my nerves became rasped to the shrieking point?

Each day the natives grew surlier and more and more sullen and intractable.

One night, not long before the full of the moon, I entered the dungeon where de Montour sat.

He looked up quickly.

"You dare much, coming to me in the night."

I shrugged my shoulders, seating myself.

A small barred window let in the night scents and sounds of Africa.

"Hark to the native drums," I said. "For the past week they have sounded almost incessantly."

De Montour assented.

"The natives are restless. Methinks 'tis deviltry they are planning. Have you noticed that Carlos is much among them?"

"No," I answered, "but 'tis like there will be a break between him and Luigi. Luigi is paying court to Ysabel."

So we talked, when suddenly de Montour became silent and moody, answering only in monosyllables.

The moon rose and peered in at the battered windows. De Montour's face was illuminated by its beams.

And then the hand of horror grasped me. On the wall behind de Montour appeared a shadow, a shadow clearly defined of a *wolf's head!*

At the same instant de Montour felt its influence. With a shriek he bounded from his stool.

He pointed fiercely, and as with trembling hands I slammed and bolted the door behind me, I felt him hurl his weight against it. As I fled up the stairway I heard a wild raving and battering at the iron-bound door. But with all the werewolf's might the great door held.

As I entered my room, Gola dashed in and gasped out the tale he had been keeping for days.

I listened, incredulously, and then dashed forth to find Dom Vincente.

I was told that Carlos had asked him to accompany him to the village to arrange a sale of slaves.

My informer was Don Florenzo of Seville, and when I gave him a brief outline of Gola's tale, he accompanied me.

Together we dashed through the castle gate, flinging a word to the guards, and down the landing toward the village.

Dom Vincente, Dom Vincente, walk with care, keep sword loosened in its sheath! Fool, fool, to walk in the night with Carlos, the traitor!

They were nearing the village when we caught up with them. "Dom Vincente!" I exclaimed; "return instantly to the castle. Carlos is selling you into the hands of the natives! Gola has told me that he lusts for your wealth and for Ysabel! A terrified native babbled to him of booted footprints near the places where the woodcutters were murdered, and Carlos has made the blacks believe that the slayer was you! Tonight the natives are to rise and slay every man in the castle except Carlos! Do you not believe me, Dom Vincente?"

"Is this truth, Carlos?" asked Dom Vincente, in amaze.

Carlos laughed mockingly.

"The fool speaks truth," he said, "but it accomplishes you nothing. Ho!"

He shouted as he leaped for Dom Vincente. Steel flashed in the moonlight and the Spaniard's sword was through Carlos ere he could move.

And the shadows rose about us. Then it was back to back, sword and dagger, three men against a hundred. Spears flashed, and a fiendish yell went up from savage throats. I spitted three natives in as many thrusts and then went down from a stunning swing from a war-club, and an instant later

Dom Vincente fell upon me, with a spear in one arm and another through the leg. Don Florenzo was standing above us, sword leaping like a living thing, when a charge of the arquebusiers swept the riverbank clear and we were borne into the castle.

The black hordes came with a rush, spears flashing like a wave of steel, a thunderous roar of savagery going up to the skies.

Time and again they swept up the slopes, bounding the moat, until they went swarming over the palisades. And time and again the fire of the hundred-odd defenders hurled them back.

They had set fire to the plundered warehouses, and their light vied with the light of the moon. Just across the river there was a larger storehouse, and about this hordes of the natives gathered, tearing it apart for plunder.

"Would that they would drop torch upon it," said Dom Vincente, "for naught is stored therein save some thousand pounds of gunpowder. I dared not store the treacherous stuff this side the river. All the tribes of the river and coast have gathered for our slaughter and all my ships are upon the seas. We may hold out awhile, but eventually they will swarm the palisade and put us to the slaughter."

I hastened to the dungeon wherein de Montour sat. Outside the door I called to him and he bade me enter in a voice which told me the fiend had left him for an instant.

"The blacks have risen," I told him.

"I guessed as much. How goes the battle?"

I gave him the details of the betrayal and the

fight, and mentioned the powder-house across the river. He sprang to his feet.

"Now by my hag-ridden soul!" he exclaimed; "I will fling the dice once more with hell! Swift, let me out of the castle! I will essay to swim the river and set off yon powder!"

"It is insanity!" I exclaimed. "A thousand blacks lurk between the palisades and the river, and thrice that number beyond! The river itself swarms with crocodiles!"

"I will attempt it!" he answered, a great light in his face. "If I can reach it, some thousand natives will lighten the siege; if I am slain, then my soul is free and mayhap will gain some forgiveness for that I gave my life to atone for my crimes."

Then, "Haste," he exclaimed, "for the demon is returning! Already I feel his influence! Haste ye!"

For the castle gates we sped, and as de Montour ran he gasped as a man in a terrific battle.

At the gate he pitched headlong, then rose, to spring through it. Wild yells greeted him from the natives.

The arquebusiers shouted curses at him and at me. Peering down from the top of the palisades I saw him turn from side to side uncertainly. A score of natives were rushing recklessly forward, spears raised.

Then the eery wolf-yell rose to the skies, and de Montour bounded forward. Aghast, the natives paused, and before a man of them could move he was among them. Wild shrieks, not of rage, but of terror.

In amazement the arquebusiers held their fire. Straight through the group of blacks de Montour charged, and when they broke and fled, three of them fled not.

A dozen steps de Montour took in pursuit; then stopped stock-still. A moment he stood so, while spears flew about him, then turned and ran swiftly in the direction of the river.

A few steps from the river another band of blacks barred his way. In the flaming light of the burning houses the scene was clearly illuminated. A thrown spear tore through de Montour's shoulder. Without pausing in his stride he tore it forth and drove it through a native, leaping over his body to get among the others.

They could not face the fiend-driven white man. With shrieks they fled, and de Montour, bounding upon the back of one, brought him down.

Then he rose, staggered and sprang to the riverbank. An instant he paused there and then vanished into the shadows.

"Name of the devil!" gasped Dom Vincente at my shoulder. "What manner of man is that? Was that de Montour?"

I nodded. The wild yells of the natives rose above the crackle of the arquebus fire. They were massed thick about the great warehouse across the river.

"They plan a great rush," said Dom Vincente. "They will swarm clear over the palisade, me thinks. Ha!"

A crash that seemed to rip the skies apart! A burst of flame that mounted to the stars! The castle rocked with the explosion. Then silence, as the smoke, drifting away, showed only a great crater where the warehouse had stood.

I could tell of how Dom Vincente led a charge, crippled as he was, out of the castle gate and down the slope, to fall upon the terrified blacks who had escaped the explosion. I could tell of the slaughter, of the victory and the pursuit of the fleeing natives.

I could tell, too, *Messieurs*, of how I became separated from the band and of how I wandered far into the jungle, unable to find my way back to the coast.

I could tell how I was captured by a wandering band of slave raiders, and of how I escaped. But such is not my intention. In itself it would make a long tale; and it is of de Montour that I am speaking.

I thought much of the things that had passed and wondered if indeed de Montour reached the storehouse to blow it to the skies or whether it was but the deed of chance.

That a man could swim that reptile-swarming river, fiend-driven though he was, seemed impossible. And if he blew up the storehouse, he must have gone up with it.

So one night I pushed my way wearily through the jungle and sighted the coast, and close to the shore a small, tumble-down hut of thatch. To it I went, thinking to sleep therein if insects and reptiles would allow.

I entered the doorway and then stopped short. Upon a makeshift stool sat a man. He looked up as I entered and the rays of the moon fell across his face.

I started back with a ghastly thrill of horror. *It was de Montour, and the moon was full!*

Then as I stood, unable to flee, he rose and

came toward me. And his face, though haggard as of a man who has looked into hell, was the face of a sane man.

"Come in, my friend," he said, and there was a great peace in his voice. "Come in and fear me not. The fiend has left me forever."

"But tell me, how conquered you?" I exclaimed as I grasped his hand.

"I fought a frightful battle, as I ran to the river," he answered, "for the fiend had me in its grasp and drove me to fall upon the natives. But for the first time my soul and mind gained ascendency for an instant, an instant just long enough to hold me to my purpose. And I believe the good saints came to my aid, for I was giving my life to save life.

"I leaped into the river and swam, and in an instant the crocodiles were swarming about me.

"Again in the clutch of the fiend I fought them, there in the river. Then suddenly the *thing* left me.

"I climbed from the river and fired the warehouse. The explosion hurled me hundreds of feet, and for days I wandered witless through the jungle.

"But the full moon came, and came again, and I felt not the influence of the fiend.

"I am free, free!" And a wondrous note of exultation, nay, *exaltation*, thrilled his words:

"My soul is free. Incredible as it seems, the demon lies drowned upon the bed of the river, or else inhabits the body of one of the savage reptiles that swim the ways of the Niger."

ANNOUNCING:
THE ARCANA

A GROUNDBREAKING NEW SERIES FROM THE BESTSELLING AUTHOR OF *LION OF IRELAND!*

They are **The Arcana.** Collectively, they are the ultimate symbols of cosmic power. Millennia ago they were the treasures of the gods of creation, honored and cherished in four great cities since swept away by the rivers of time. The Spear of Light came from Gorias. The city of Falias contained The Stone of Destiny. From Murias came The Cup of Blood. The Sword of Flame was enshrined within Findias.

Properly used by an adept, these four together have the power to create worlds—or to destroy them. The three volumes of The Arcana by Morgan Llywelyn and Michael Scott tell of the desperate quest to rediscover the ancient tools of creation and restore a world that lives only in memory. A world everyone longs to return to, in their most secret dreams. The lost world at the outermost limit of human desire.

Book One tells the story of Silverhand, he who was foretold, he who is destined to save the world from Chaos and begin the long climb back to the world that lives within us all.